Well, if Tom [barcode] **of free**

MW01532475

I could remind him about responsibility and everyday reality.

I pulled into the parking lot just as T. C. was climbing into his pickup. He waved my stranded customer over and gave me a thumbs-up sign as we backed our separate vehicles out onto Exchange Street.

"Thanks," I shouted. "I'll cook you dinner in return."

"Monday?"

"Monday's good with me. How about seven o'clock?"

He nodded and adjusted the sunglasses he'd settled on his aquiline nose. He was as eye-catchingly handsome as he'd been thirty years earlier, I thought. And more willing than I'd expected to do a favor for a damsel in distress.

When he disappeared from my life again, I began to revise that opinion.

Dear Reader,

Happy Holidays, 1996, and welcome back to the world of Rita Magritte and her tow truck in this fourth Literacy Volunteers of Orange-Athol novel by Cathy Stanton. This year, Rita reencounters an old flame.

Cathy writes as Cathryn Clare for Silhouette Books, New York. An Athol resident, she carries on this very appropriate fundraising plan as a salute both to fun and literacy while honoring generous businesses and individuals in the North Quabbin area.

Cathy's interest in Literacy Volunteers extended naturally from her longtime service to the organization as tutor and coordinator.

As Cathy's publication list reveals, she is a writer of varied talents with fourteen Silhouette novels to her credit. She is also a playwright and has contributed to a range of periodical publications.

Oh, yes. And, as Cathy has promised, *Trouble on the Wing* is just the fourth in the continuing series about Rita Magritte. So, just wait till next year.

Board of Directors
Literacy Volunteers of Orange-Athol

CATHY STANTON

TROUBLE ON THE WING

**LITERACY VOLUNTEERS
OF ORANGE-ATHOL**

PUBLISHED BY HALEY'S
ATHOL, MASSACHUSETTS

LITERACY VOLUNTEERS
OF ORANGE-ATHOL
in cooperation with HALEY'S
Post Office Box 248
Athol, MA   01331

TROUBLE ON THE WING

International Standard Book Number: 1-884540-25-2
Library of Congress Catalogue Number: 96-078628

First Edition. First Printing. November 1996.

All the characters in this book have no existence outside the imagination of the author, except as permission has otherwise been received, and have no relation whatsoever to anyone bearing the same name or names. They are not even distantly inspired by any individual known or unknown to the author, except as permission has been received, and all incidents are pure invention.

Book and cover design by Mary Pat Spaulding.
Cover photography by Robert Mayer.
Caricatures by Bill LaRose.
Copy read by Marcia Gagliardi and Dorothy Hayden.
Layout formatted in Aldus Pagemaker 6.0.
Imagemaking and printing by The Highland Press.

Special thanks to Carol Lauriat.

Also by Cathy Stanton

Romantic Suspense Novels
> written using the pseudonym *Cathryn Clare*
> for *Silhouette Intimate Moments*

A Marriage to Remember, scheduled July 1997
The Baby Assignment, July 1996
The Honeymoon Assignment, May 1996
The Wedding Assignment, March 1996
Gunslinger's Child, March 1995
The Angel and the Renegade, October 1994
Sun and Shadow, March 1994
Chasing Destiny, June 1993

Romance Novels
> written using the pseudonym *Cathryn Clare*
> for *Silhouette Desire*

Hot Stuff, January 1992
The Midas Touch, September 1991
Five by Ten, September 1990
Lock, Stock and Barrel, September 1990
Blind Justice, July 1989
To the Highest Bidder, January 1988

Short Mystery Fiction
Multiple Submissions, **Alfred Hitchcock's Mystery Magazine,**
September 1989
The Teddy Bears' Wake, **Alfred Hitchcock's Mystery Magazine,**
August 1988

The *Trouble* series
> for *Literacy Volunteers of Orange-Athol* and *Haley's*

Trouble by the Pound, November 1995
Trouble in Tandem, November 1994
Trouble in Tow, November 1993

CATHY STANTON

was born in Canada in 1958. She worked for several years in Toronto as a flutist, singer, and storyteller. She was an arts administrator before moving to the Boston area in 1983. She and her husband Fred Holmgren, a classical trumpet player, have lived in Athol since 1988, and Cathy has been a full-time writer since then. Her novels have been translated into ten languages and have sold more than a million copies worldwide.

She has also pursued an interest in theatre. Her plays have been staged in Toronto and at Gettysburg College, Pennsylvania, and given readings in Boston and New York.

She has been involved in Literacy Volunteers of America since 1988. She is also a member of Romance Writers of America, and she is currently pursuing a master's degree in anthropology through Vermont College in Montpelier.

For Dottie Hayden,
with affection.

ACKNOWLEDGMENTS

This book is truly a cooperative effort. Aside from the fact that it could not be produced at all without the support of the sponsors whose names appear in the story, there are several important contributors who play an invisible but crucial part in the ongoing Rita Magritte series.

The Highland Press generously underwrites the project by donating a part of the printing cost. Pat Spaulding of Spaulding Graphics graciously and professionally designs the book. And Marcia Gagliardi of Haley's makes it all happen by editing the manuscript and coordinating production with efficiency and good humor. Rita Magritte takes shape in my imagination, but the support and expertise of all these people are necessary to get her off the ground.

Pat Smith and Carole Brennan at the Literacy Volunteers of Orange-Athol office provided invaluable help this year, as always. I'm grateful, too, to Derek Estler for furnishing information and to Baker School Specialty in Orange, which made a substantial donation to this year's book. Finally, I want to thank my husband Fred, who has helped me with all my plots—including this one—at one time or another.

Cathy Stanton

ONE

"So why exactly were you in jail?"

All evening I'd been trying to find a good way to work the question in. Finally, between the ordering of dessert and the arrival of coffee, I'd found a good opening—or so I'd thought.

T. C.'s big laugh turned heads at all the tables around us and told me my attempt to be subtle hadn't worked.

"You haven't changed, Rita," he told me, leaning back in his chair. "You've got that same look on your face that you used to have when you asked me what I was planning to do with my life after high school."

"Drat," I said. "And here I was trying to be so casual."

He laughed again. It was impossible—always had been impossible—not to laugh along with him. "I'll give you a tip," he said. "Don't try so hard—it'll work better."

It was advice from a master. Tom Carter, known to his friends as T. C., had a natural nonchalance that had always been astonishingly seductive. His nickname was appropriate. There was a tomcat slinkiness to him, a half-tamed charm that had captivated more hearts than just mine.

"Was I that obvious back in high school?" I asked him. "About wanting to know what your plans were, I mean."

His long mouth tilted in a grin. "You were looking out for yourself," he said. "In my experience, that's what women want—security, stability, all that stuff."

I didn't allow myself to speculate about how many women T. C.'s experience included. His once-black hair had turned to silver, and his lean face was etched with the crow's feet that all pilots seem to get from squinting into the sun. But he was as handsome as ever, especially when he smiled.

It was beginning to occur to me that it felt like a very long time since a man had smiled at me that way.

We were sharing the evening at the Homestead Restaurant in Orange. He'd called me after work—as he'd been doing fre-

1

quently since returning to his hometown—and invited me to spend some time with him. Since my own work schedule was light, I'd said yes. And now, after a thoroughly pleasant ramble through the woods in New Salem, we were having dinner at the Homestead.

I liked the comfortable, country atmosphere of the restaurant, with its antiques and old photos filling every nook and cranny and its strings of tiny lights making the low-ceilinged rooms glow gently. And I liked the man I was sitting across from.

Although I'd accumulated a lot of age and experience since the days when I'd been head over heels in love with Tom Carter, there was no denying that even at fifty there were still some sparks flying between us. I could feel them sizzling as I met his eyes and smiled back at him.

"My daughter Hannah doesn't think I want security and stability," I said. "She's convinced I'm the world's most bohemian and irresponsible middle-aged female, just because I chose to keep the towing business going after Henry died. As far as she's concerned, I don't have an ounce of propriety in my entire body."

I couldn't help noticing the way T. C.'s eyes roved over my body as I referred to it. Ample though my fifty-year-old frame might be, to my astonishment it still seemed to catch his eye as it had done when we were both seventeen.

I was just as astonished by my own response to the suggestive glint in his blue eyes. Even the mention of my late husband Henry, who'd died almost ten years earlier, wasn't enough to keep my feet on the ground and my imagination under control.

"It must drive her crazy that you're hanging out with me, then," T. C. said.

"Oh, it does. Just the other day she asked me very pointedly whether I intended to act my age once I become a grandmother. I'd just told her you'd taken me for a romantic sunset flight over the Quabbin Reservoir, and she was scandalized. Apparently grandmothers don't do that kind of thing."

The waitress returned with our coffee and dessert—apple pie for me, chocolate cheesecake for T. C., who looked as though he hadn't gained an ounce since he'd walked out of high school to join the Air Force thirty-three years earlier.

His face was more serious, though, as he leaned back toward me when the waitress had gone. "It's September, right, that Hannah's baby's due?" he asked.

"That's right."

He tilted his silver head. "It's an appealing thought," he said. "Grandchildren, I mean." Then that stray-cat gleam came back into his blue eyes. "Much more appealing than the idea of having children," he added.

I shook my head at him. "It's hard to have one without the other, T. C."

"I know." His grin was unrepentant. "There's always a catch, isn't there?"

I sipped my coffee and ate some pie. The Homestead was packed with customers, as it always was on Thursday evenings. But we were in a quiet corner toward the back. Just at the moment, the murmur of conversations going on all around us seemed muted and distant.

When I'd satisfied myself that the pie was up to the Homestead's usual standards, I leaned back against the wall of our booth and said, "So why *were* you in jail, anyway?"

His light laugh told me he'd been hoping I'd forgotten my original question. "That's the catch with you, Rita, isn't it?" he said. "You never let go of things until you've figured them out."

He reached across the table and took my free hand, looking down at my plain, square fingers. There was nothing beautiful about my hands—no polish, no diamond ring—but T. C. seemed fascinated by the sight of my fingers entwining with his own.

I hadn't let go of Tom Carter thirty-three years earlier, I thought. He'd just flown away out of my life, leaving me brokenhearted and convinced I would never love anyone again.

Henry Magritte had proved me wrong. I suppose, in retrospect, that Henry caught me on the rebound, proposing to me almost exactly a year after T. C. had run off to join the Air Force. But we'd had a happy marriage until Henry's sudden death in 1987. We'd been good partners in marriage, in parenthood, in the business we'd built up together. We'd been compatible in a way that I still missed.

The fact that I missed Henry, though, wasn't enough to keep my blood from humming when T. C. gently stroked the back of my hand with his thumb.

"I figured you'd have read all about it in the papers," he said. "Local boy screws up—again."

I reclaimed my hand, because I could already feel my common sense eroding around the edges. T. C. had always been as good at ducking questions as I was at asking them, but I'd be damned if I was going to let him slide out from under this one, no matter how much I enjoyed the feeling of his hand holding mine.

"I hate to burst your bubble, T. C.," I said, "but it wasn't exactly a front-page item. I remember something about a police raid—"

"It wasn't a raid. Just a pair of cops trying to bust up a bar fight."

"Which you had started, I assume."

He grinned. "Not exactly," he said. "But I didn't waste any time getting into it. A couple of guys jumped my buddy Rick. I was trying to give him a hand."

"And you hit one of the cops instead."

"Yeah. Real hard, as it turned out." He took a couple of bites of his cheesecake, then pushed the plate a little closer to my side of the table. "This is outstanding cheesecake, Rita. Help yourself to—"

"T. C." I smiled at him. "The fight?"

He had the grace to look sheepish. "Yeah, well, it was a mess," he said. "Rick and I liked to get together whenever I was in town. We'd been reminiscing about old times—we were in Vietnam together. And we'd hoisted a few drinks, so I was kind of—" He hesitated.

"Loaded," I supplied helpfully.

"Well, yeah. It was one of those don't-know-my-own-strength things. And it didn't help my case that the cop's jaw was still wired together when he gave his testimony at my trial. Made kind of a bad impression on the jury."

"But you still only served six months."

He shrugged and took another big bite of his dessert. "First offense," he said. "Hell, Rick got off with a suspended sentence. Of course, he hit the right guys. I always was unlucky."

Two tours in Vietnam, a stint in a POW camp, twenty years of flying in the Alaskan bush, several hair-raisingly close emergency landings—he'd told me enough stories over the past week and a half that I was convinced he really was a tomcat, or at least he had as many lives as one.

"You're not unlucky," I told him sternly. "Reckless, yes. Impulsive, definitely. But you've had more than your share of luck, T. C. I'm just amazed it took you this long to land in jail."

His grin was rueful. "Thanks," he said. "I think." He finished his cheesecake and took a sip of coffee. "The ironic thing is that the prison sentence was a milk run compared with the way parole is shaping up."

He'd already told me about the hard-line parole officer he'd drawn. The two of them had taken an instant dislike to one another.

"Is he still dropping in on you every other day?" I asked.

"Try *every* day. It's like living with my mother again—except she didn't have the authority to dump me back in jail if I irritated her. And everything I do irritates this guy. I had to call him to tell him I was leaving work early today. He wanted to know where I was going. For a walk with a friend, I said. Well, who was the friend? I told him it was none of his business."

"I bet that went over well."

"Oh, you bet. So I had to give him your name, or he'd have been breathing down my neck all evening."

This was news to me, and not entirely welcome news. It was one thing to scandalize Hannah by keeping company with the town's perennial bad boy. I was used to my daughter being outraged by my behavior.

But knowing that an official of the state corrections department was keeping tabs on what I was up to with T. C.—well. *That* was another story.

I shook my head. This *was* like old times, I thought. The renegade thrill of being with Tom Carter had always been tinged with the all-too-real possibility of trouble.

"He must have come around," I said. "You haven't had to spend the evening calling in to report where you are, like you did on our first date."

"No." He drained his coffee cup. He did everything that way, I recalled. He didn't sip things—he swallowed them whole. It summed up his whole approach to life. He'd always been hungry for adventure, for experience. And he was frequently impatient with the consequences.

"But I did have to ask for a receipt from the woman at the bookstore, if you recall," he added. "And I'll have to get another one from the Homestead, just to prove I was really here."

I'd wondered at his request when we'd bought a copy of an old high school yearbook from the Common Reader Bookshop in New Salem. We'd stopped there after our walk, spending a happy hour perusing the shelves of old books. We'd stopped to pat a pair of small dogs belonging to the owners, who'd explained that the older dog dozing under a table was named Amelia Dearheart, while the younger, livelier pup was Della Sweet.

The store was a comfortable, unhurried kind of place, and we'd had a good time there, especially when we'd discovered

Common Reader Bookshop

an old high school yearbook with our own impossibly young-looking pictures in it.

It was a typical T. C. move to buy it, saying he wanted it to remind him of his not-so-glorious roots. It had not, however, been typical of him to ask the woman who'd taken his money for a receipt with his name and the date on it.

"And here I thought you were becoming a responsible citizen in your middle age," I teased him. "I figured you'd found a way to make all this tax-deductible, and you were already thinking about next year's tax return."

His face told me how much time he spent thinking about any year's tax return. "Give me a break, Rita," he said. "In fact, that's what this is supposed to be—a break. So let's not spend it talking about my friendly parole officer. Sun's going down, in case you hadn't noticed. If you don't hurry up and finish that pie, we're going to miss the show."

Just to make sure we didn't, he helped me with the last of my dessert. Then we hurried over to the Orange Airport, where T. C., ever the smooth operator, had managed to get the local parachute club to let him use one of their single-engine planes during off-hours in exchange for his services as a pilot when they were busy. It was becoming a nightly ritual for the two of us to lift off into the air and follow the setting sun as it sank into the western sky.

That was what I had loved about T. C.—his drop-everything, savor-the-moment approach to life.

It was also the thing that had bothered me most about him. I'd never decided whether I wanted to throw caution to the wind and go with him, or whether I was happiest, after all, with the life I'd made at home.

Over the course of the next few days, I was going to have plenty of opportunity to answer that question once and for all.

TWO

"And then the border will coordinate with the mobile over the crib. With all those different colors, it won't matter whether we end up with pink or blue sheets."

There was a light breeze wafting across the porch at Ralph Longg's Marketplace. I stretched my legs out and enjoyed the sensation of it. The June day was perfect, crystal-clear, warm in the sun, cool in the shade. I was full of good food and iced tea, and part of my mind was still wafting along in thoughts of how the sky had looked last night as T. C. and I had skimmed above the golden surface of the Quabbin Reservoir at sunset.

In short, I wasn't paying attention.

"Mom." The annoyance in Hannah's voice brought me back to reality. "Are you even listening to me?"

I blinked and realized I'd closed my eyes as I basked in the breeze. I was feeling like a cat, I thought—a big, broad old tabby cat suddenly finding herself rejuvenated by the reappearance of the beat-up old tom she'd thought had slunk out of town long ago.

"I'm sorry, honey," I said. "What were you saying?"

It turned out to be variations on the same theme Hannah had been working on ever since she'd learned she was pregnant. Everything had to be just right before the baby was born—and that meant an amount of shopping and reorganizing and redecorating that had me feeling exhausted four months before the happy event.

She'd put down a sample of a wallpaper border on the table between us. I looked at the bright teddy-bear pattern and tried to feel fascinated.

Judging by the look on Hannah's face, I wasn't very successful. "Didn't you go through this before Mike and I were born?" she asked, sounding a little plaintive.

"To be honest, honey, your father and I were so busy trying to make room for the stuff we'd had to clear out of the spare

Ralph Longg's Marketplace

rooms that we didn't have time for much extra fussing," I said. "You know how tiny that house was—is."

Even now, with Henry gone and the two kids grown up and moved out, my house was none too spacious. My teenaged tenant and part-time employee took up a lot of the room these days. So did my oversized black and brown watchdog, whom I'd been letting inside the house more and more often since I'd almost lost him the previous autumn.

Hannah had always made it clear that she wanted a big house of her own. Now that her husband Jim had a new job as a foreman at Baker School Specialty in the Orange Industrial Park, and Hannah's own career as a bank teller was going well, they'd built a big addition on their home.

I think sometimes she wished she could alter me as easily. Her friends' mothers would have been in raptures over the tiny print on the wallpaper borders, her disappointed expression was telling me.

"I think you might want to save a few things for your friends to buy for your shower," I said carefully.

"Oh, that's no problem." Her face cleared instantly. "I made a list of what we still need, and Nerissa made sure everybody who was invited to the shower got a copy."

She glanced at her watch and lifted her purse from the seat next to her. "I've got to get back to work. Now, are you sure you're all organized for the shower?"

"I'm as organized as I'm going to get."

I still wasn't sure how I'd been maneuvered into acting as co-hostess for Hannah's baby shower, scheduled for the following Friday evening. I had a sneaking suspicion that Hannah and her friend Nerissa thought the experience would be good for me. As I result, I'd been digging my heels in slightly whenever the subject of the shower came up.

"You've got the dessert things under control?"

"Hannah, who made your school lunches for sixteen years worth of school?"

She rolled her eyes at me in a way that made her look suddenly less like an expectant young matron and more like the prim and proper child she'd once been. "I know," she said. "It's just—"

"And didn't you always have homemade cookies in those lunches?"

"You're not going to make *cookies*, are you?" She sounded shocked. "This is going to be a big gathering, Mom. I was hoping—"

I squeezed her hand. "Hannah," I said. "Don't worry. I won't disgrace you. And I won't bring cookies. You'll just have to trust that I'll come up with the right thing."

She still looked dubious as we paid our check and walked down off the porch into the June sunshine flooding the yard. "I heard from my friend at the Homestead that you and Tom Carter were in there for supper last night," she said.

Small towns, I thought. *No wonder T. C. wanted to get out of this fishbowl atmosphere.*

"He's an old friend, honey," I said. "I enjoy his company."

"Mom, he's a convicted felon!"

"Who's served his time—all six months of it."

"Why did he come back here, anyway?"

"I told you. His mother died. He inherited her house. And now that he's on parole, he needs a permanent address and a stable job for the next two years. Getting a job was one of the conditions of his getting out at all. Ledgard's Warehouse was willing to hire him, so he took them up on it."

Hannah didn't look happy with any of my answers. "You're not—having an *affair* with him or anything, are you?" she asked.

I looked around me. Despite the melodramatic undertones in Hannah's voice we were still in downtown Main Street in Athol, not Peyton Place.

"Hannah," I said, "let's make a deal. I'll try to take more of an interest in your baby plans, if you'll try to take *less* of one in my romantic life. How does that sound?"

Her expression told me she wasn't happy about it. Or maybe it was the idea of her mother having a romantic life at all that was bothering her. We'd reached some kind of truce by the time we parted on the sidewalk. But it was an uneasy one, and it was enough to knock the shine off the perfect day as I climbed up into my wrecker and went back to work.

The Jumptown Parachute Club had just recently moved into the Orange Airport, occupying part of one of the hangars that faced the main runway. There were several other businesses based at the airport, most of them marketing their services for charter flights, land surveying, flying lessons, and other airborne ventures. T. C. seemed to know everybody, and he'd introduced me to most of the pilots and businesspeople in the short time since I'd been joining him for our evening flights. I waved to one of those people, the owner of Mehr Aviation, as I passed the company's plane in the hangar next to Jumptown's. As a longtime neighbor of the airport, I knew that parachuting had a history there. The nation's first commercial parachute operation, in fact, had opened in Orange in 1959.

Jumptown members were at the airport during most of the daylight hours on weekends and holidays, T. C. had told me, and they'd been pleased to have a pilot of his skill and experience join them. The club owned a couple of single-engine planes and contracted with independent pilots during their busy times to take jumpers up.

On a beautiful long June evening like this one, there'd been a steady stream of parachutists floating down out of the blue sky. T. C., a man outside the Jumptown office told me, was still up on a run.

"But he'll be back any time now," he added. "Sun's going down, so we're starting to pack up for the day."

T. C. loved to fly during this brief time between sunset and night. His first phone call to me after our thirty-three year silence, in fact, had been an invitation to come and watch the sunset with him. Since then, I'd been flying with him every night.

He played the ace pilot role to the hilt. Not contented with mere sunglasses, he wore goggles when he flew and a vener-

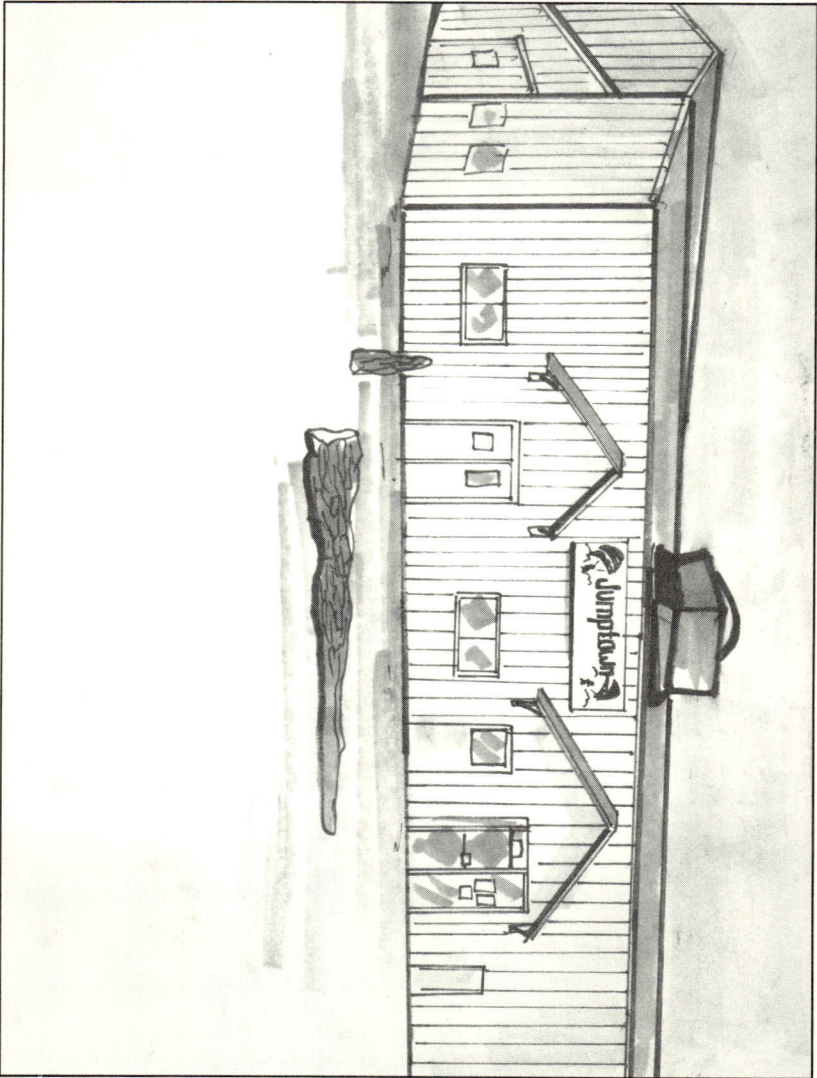

Jumptown

able old baseball cap pulled down over his silver hair. He looked like something out of a World War I recruiting poster. All that was missing was the white silk scarf, and I was half-thinking of buying him one to complete the picture.

T. C. had also told me the club held night jumps on weekends when there was a full moon. Wearing high-visibility lights, jumpers would drop out into the darkness, something I couldn't imagine doing even if someone were holding a gun to my head.

I watched a pair of brightly-colored parachutes billowing out above two jumpers who were almost ready to touch down at the far end of the airport field. "Tell me again how fast a free-fall is," I said to the man outside the office.

"About a hundred and twenty miles an hour." His face wore an expression I recognized. It was half delight at astonishing a non-jumper like me and half excitement at recalling that free-fall thrill.

Maybe it was something else, too. "You should try it," he added, as both of us turned to watch the two nearby parachutists making their surprisingly graceful landings on the field. "We get a lot of first-time jumpers here. There's nothing like it, believe me."

What was it about daredevils, I wondered, that made them so eager to pull ordinary people like me over the edge of new experiences? T. C. had always been that way, cajoling me years ago into climbing Mount Monadnock with him in the dark so we could watch the sun rise, insisting that I ride with him on his motorcycle so I could feel the thrill of pushing the machine to its maximum speed on a winding country road.

Left on my own, I would never seek out those thrills. But I could almost understand how they got to be habit-forming. The gleam in the club member's eyes told me he was already thinking of his next jump and feeling the adrenaline rush of stepping out of the plane into thin air with nothing between him and the hard ground but some silk and string.

"Thanks," I said. "But just going up in a plane is enough of a thrill for me."

And the plane I was waiting for was coming in for a landing at that moment. I watched as the little blue and yellow craft circled around to the east, then approached the runway.

"T. C. a friend of yours?" the Jumptown man asked me.

I nodded.

"He's a hell of a flyer. We've got some good pilots here, but nobody else with T. C.'s kind of chops. Did you know he used to be a regional aerobatics champion?"

I hadn't, but very little surprised me about Tom Carter anymore. "There's an aerobatics competition here every year, right?" I asked.

"Right. T. C. just missed this year's show. He'll clean up next year, though, if he decides to enter. I've seen him out there practicing, and he's got the kind of control most people just dream about. Watch this, now." He nodded toward the plane that T. C. was guiding onto the runway. "This boy's got a golden touch on the rudder."

"Not just on the rudder," I muttered, as I moved toward the runway to meet the little blue and yellow plane as it cruised to a silken-smooth landing and taxied toward the building. I was thinking about T. C.'s good-night kiss the night before. And it was fortunate, given the way my cheeks flamed at the recollection, that the man from Jumptown had already turned away to attend to something else.

T. C. was fiddling with the control panel when I reached the plane. He reached behind him to open the passenger door for me, but almost immediately he went back to flicking one of the gauges with his middle finger.

"Everything okay?" I asked.

"Sure." He had to raise his voice to be heard over the noise of the engine. "Nothing major." I could tell from his manner, though, that something about the plane's performance was bothering him. The curve of his mouth under his silver moustache looked tense, as if his concentration was elsewhere.

"We don't have to—"

He didn't let me finish. Swinging one long arm over the back of his seat, he put a hand over mine as I adjusted my seatbelt. "It's fine," he reiterated. "Don't want to miss the show."

And we didn't. The whole western sky turned orange as we swung in the now-familiar route over the reservoir. The last rays of the sun faded on the clear surface of the water far below us.

Afterward, T. C. hollered over his shoulder that he still hadn't been able to get the gauge to work properly, and he wanted to fix it before his boss needed the plane the next day. So I settled for a quick shouted good-night over the roar of the engine, instead of the lingering kiss I'd secretly been hoping for and walked home wondering why it felt as though T. C. and I had been soaring up into the air to watch the sunset every night for years, instead of just for a week.

Saturday's schedule was a reality check.

It started before dawn with a call from the state police about an accident on Route 2 in Phillipston. The driver had apparently fallen asleep at the wheel and gone down the embankment head first in fifth gear. They'd taken him to the hospital by the time I arrived. I could hear the thump-thump of the Lifeflight helicopter landing in Athol as I pulled the crumpled Chevy out of the ditch.

The state cops and I all wore the same expression. People who see a lot of death and disaster get that way—hushed in the presence of destruction, respectful of the fact that each of us, at any time, could be the one going over the edge.

That was how adventures ended at least half the time, I thought. It was all very well to feel seduced by the outlaw thrill of Tom Carter's laughing blue eyes when I was standing close to him and feeling the heat of his hand wrapped around mine. But life was earnest. Life was real. And it never seemed more real than right after an early morning tow call to pull some twisted wreck out of a ditch.

I'd barely had time to get home and get the coffee started before my second call of the day came in. I recognized the tone of voice right away—politely desperate.

"If you can just tow me to somewhere where somebody could take a look at it," the woman said, "I think it's something to do with the plugs."

The vagueness of her directions told me this wasn't a local driver. By the time she found a mechanic willing to squeeze her into his Saturday morning schedule, I thought, she was going to be very late getting to where she was going.

She was headed for a conference, she told me as I hooked up her car. She worked for a literacy program in Boston. She'd had a few days off to visit friends in New York state, but now she was on her way back for the annual conference, which was beginning—she checked her watch—in just over an hour.

"Literacy Volunteers, huh?" I said, as I pushed the switch to hoist the vehicle's front end off the pavement. "I've heard of them. There's a local chapter here—my old second-grade teacher used to run it."

Desperation was starting to edge out the politeness in the young woman's tone. She obviously didn't want to chat about my second-grade teacher. "If I could just rent a car or something," she kept saying. "My workshop's not until eleven—I could still get there in time."

I towed her to Newcomb Motors, which was the nearest Plymouth dealership. They were willing to have a look at the problem, but—like the other garages she called from their office—they couldn't guarantee she would be back on the road in time.

Hannah thinks I'm not sufficiently motherly, but she's wrong. My motherly qualities are just aroused by situations that Hannah takes good care never to get herself into. And the sight of the anxious young woman trying unsuccessfully to find a rental car or a mechanic made me feel I couldn't just drive off and leave her. I could tell how important it was to the literacy woman to get to her conference on time.

So, I pitched in. I called my son Mike, who's a self-employed mechanic, and explained the problem. "Newcomb's your best bet," he said. "But she won't be anywhere by eleven, even if they have the part in stock."

The young woman was starting to droop as I relayed the news to her. She was at the end of her options, I thought. Fortunately, I wasn't.

"Listen," I said. "I have a friend who's going into Boston anyway today." It was true. T. C. had told me on Thursday that he planned to spend Saturday and Sunday visiting his friend Rick. He'd cleared it with his parole officer, after a series of promises and conditions that he said made the average prenuptial agreement look slap-dash by comparison.

So if T. C. was heading east anyway, why couldn't he give the woman from Literacy Volunteers a lift? In the back of my mind, as I dialed his number, I could hear his amused voice saying *That's what women want—security, stability, all that stuff.* Probably he thought we all just wanted to be rescued when our cars broke down, too—those of us not already driving fully-equipped wreckers, that is.

Well, if Tom Carter could give me a taste of freedom and adventure, I could remind him about responsibility and everyday reality. And he didn't sound displeased by my request, just a little groggy, as though I'd wakened him.

He agreed readily enough to do the young woman a favor, and suggested that I drop her off at Star Donuts in Athol, since he wanted to lay in a supply of doughnuts and coffee before heading into the city.

I pulled into the parking lot—which the doughnut shop shared with Tool Town Pizza—just as T. C. was climbing into his pickup. He waved my stranded customer over and gave me a thumbs-up sign as we backed our separate vehicles out onto Exchange Street.

"Thanks," I shouted. "I'll cook you dinner in return."

"Monday?"

"Monday's good with me. How about seven o'clock?"

He nodded and adjusted the sunglasses he'd settled on his aquiline nose. He was as eye-catchingly handsome as he'd been thirty years earlier, I thought. And more willing than I'd expected to do a favor for a damsel in distress.

When he disappeared from my life again, I began to revise that opinion.

THREE

T. C.'s father died the year after Henry did. The event brought T. C. back from the wilds of Alaska, where he'd been a bush pilot for years. He'd been married briefly while he was up there, he'd told me, but it hadn't lasted. He was alone when he came back to Massachusetts to help his mother cope with his father's sudden death.

Rocked by my own recent loss and by the overwhelming task of trying to keep the towing business running on my own, I'd barely noticed his return. And he hadn't stayed long. He'd attended the old man's memorial service and helped his younger brother Casey arrange for their ailing mother to move into the Quabbin Valley Convalescent Center.

Then, he'd gone again. He'd headed up to northern Maine because it was the closest thing to wilderness that New England offered. He'd been an unexpectedly dutiful son, returning twice a year to visit his mother on Christmas and her birthday. But he hadn't shown any signs of putting down roots in the area until his mother's death the previous winter—and his own need for a home and a job while he was on parole—brought him back for good.

At least, he said it was for good. And I happened to drive by his family home on White Pond Road during my rounds on Monday and noticed a Warner Cable truck pulled up in the driveway. T. C. had talked about having cable installed in the old place, and it looked as though he'd actually gotten around to it. For the couple of years he had to spend on parole, anyway, he seemed to be reconciled to the idea of living in his old hometown.

But he never showed up for dinner on Monday evening.

At first, I wasn't concerned. T. C. was cavalier about time. He'd told me jokingly that his being late for his own wedding had been the first nail in the coffin for his brief marriage.

My erratic schedule sometimes made me late for things myself. So I was prepared to cut him some slack when he didn't show up for dinner on the stroke of seven.

By eight, I was beginning to be slightly annoyed.

By nine, I was cursing myself for a fool.

It wasn't just that I'd been stood up, though that was bad enough. But I'd fussed over this meal—fussed as anxiously as Hannah herself might have done.

I'd cleared off the dining room table and pulled out a linen tablecloth I hadn't used in years. I'd even ironed the damned thing.

I'd been acting like an eager bride, or—worse yet—a teenager playing grown-up, trying to impress a boy I had a crush on. T. C.'s reappearance had done that to me, I thought resentfully, as the hands of the clock inched slowly toward nine. I'd let myself be pulled back into a past I should have been more willing to let go.

When I'd looked through my old cookbooks, they'd seemed too familiar, too ordinary. And so I'd given in to an impulse at the end of my working day and stopped at the Hobbit Doorway bookstore in downtown Athol in search of something new and exciting.

Standing in the cookbook section in the center of the store, I'd found a volume that seemed like just the right thing. It was a hardcover book, but I justified the expense by telling myself the fruit-filled crêpes and petits-fours in the dessert section would be just the thing for Hannah's baby shower on Friday.

It was the mushroom-stuffed chicken breasts that really caught my eye, though. T. C. loved mushrooms. I'd found some dried Italian mushrooms at the supermarket, soaked them in red wine, and made a filling that was still sitting ready to be stuffed into boneless chicken breasts at nine o'clock, when I finally gave up on T. C.

"I'm not going to pick up the phone and call him," I muttered, as I scraped the stuffing into a Tupperware container. "He can call me, when he remembers I exist."

Chili Dog, my big black and brown mutt, was watching with interest from his corner of the kitchen. He tilted his broad head when I spoke, as though he was trying to figure out what the tone of my voice meant.

What it meant was that I was kicking myself for forgetting how unreliable Tom Carter could be. "Tomcat indeed," I said. "Hound dog, is more like it. Come on, Chili, this is your lucky day."

It gave me perverse satisfaction to feed Chili a couple of the slices of French bread with olive paste I'd planned to impress T. C. with. He wagged his stumpy tail in appreciation, and I tried to tell myself I was just as happy with the company of my dog and my own quiet house.

But the truth was that I'd been looking forward to T. C.'s easy charm, his suggestive smile. And as the clock hands crept past nine-thirty, I had to admit I was a little worried about him, too.

He was the most reckless person I knew. And I couldn't help thinking of the wrecked car I'd pulled out of the ditch on Saturday. What if something had happened to T. C.?

By ten I was worried enough to swallow my pride and dial his phone number—the same number I'd committed to memory back in my lovestruck high school days.

After two rings, I heard the click of the answering machine picking up. T. C.'s deep voice, laced with the laughter I'd always found so irresistible, said, "According to the Commonwealth of Massachusetts, I'm not supposed to be far from home right now. So if you leave a message, I'm sure I'll get back to you soon."

I left a message—a brief, noncommittal inquiry about where he was.

When he hadn't called me back twenty-four hours later, I decided it was time to do something.

T. C.'s family had lived on White Pond Road in Athol for three generations. His grandfather had built the place, a low clapboard structure, painted red, that always seemed too small for T. C.'s restless energy.

The weather turned gray on Tuesday. White Pond was a flat sheet of slate when I drove the wrecker toward it at about seven P. M. It had been a long day. I'd spent the last part of it wrestling with a junker that someone had abandoned in the municipal parking lot behind Plotkin's Furniture in Athol. The car had literally fallen to bits when I'd tried to hook it up, and it had taken me two full hours to get it to my lot on Airport Road in Orange.

"And it'll probably sit there for months," I grumbled as I locked the gate. Abandoned vehicles were a nuisance to everyone, especially towing companies.

T. C.'s father had always had a yard full of old cars and trucks, although the lawn was empty now. The grass was shaggy— landscaping had never been one of T. C.'s talents. But there were other signs he'd begun fixing the place up.

Aside from the new cable line running into the house, I noticed a rusty water heater sitting out with the garbage cans. He'd had Whittier Plumbing and Heating in to replace it, he'd said, adding that he was enjoying being able to get all the shampoo out of his hair before the hot water ran out.

The front door was locked, and no one answered my knock. I shaded my eyes against the reflection from the front window. I looked inside, wondering if I would see an unrepentant T. C. lounging in his favorite position in the chair that offered the best view of the pond.

Instead, I saw something that stopped me in my tracks.

The place had been turned over, literally from top to bottom. Pictures had been pulled off the walls. The drapes hung loose, as though someone had half-ripped them off their hangers. Chairs were upside-down, their legs sticking grotesquely up in the air. The sofa cushions had been strewn around the living room, their stuffing spilling out of holes gashed in the fabric. The sheet music piled on top of T. C.'s mother's old upright piano now decorated the room like oversized ticker-tape.

My quick glance into the kitchen told me that it had received the same treatment. It was as though a hurricane had hit the place. Or maybe it was worse, I thought, as I picked my way from room to room and realized how thorough the intruders had been. A shattered pane of glass in the back door told me how they'd gotten in.

In the mess, there was a deliberate destructiveness that shook me. Drawers weren't just emptied—their contents were scattered far and wide. Family photographs had been ripped out of their frames and crumpled up. T. C.'s clothes were piled in a heap in the middle of the bedroom floor and then—I could see the marks of someone's dirty boots—trampled on.

The fury in it was unmistakable—and frightening.

T. C.'s answering machine was on a small table near the front door. The table was overturned, its slender legs smashed. The body of the phone had been tossed in one direction, the receiver in another.

But the answering machine was still in one piece.

It had been ripped out of the wall so hard the jack had been pulled right off. I picked it up and tucked it into my purse, noticing as I did it how badly my hands were shaking. I hated to leave the machine sitting there, in case there was some kind of clue on the incoming tape.

My hands started to shake much worse when I heard the screen door creaking open right behind me.

There wasn't time to wonder who it was. I barely had a chance to get to my feet before I was grabbed from behind.

"Hey!" My protesting yell was instinctive.

And useless.

Something was thrown over my face—a coat, perhaps, judging by the weight of it and the faint smell of body odor. A pair of powerful arms pinned my own arms against my sides, making it impossible to fight back.

I aimed a blind kick behind me and felt the heel of my heavy work boot connect with someone's leg. A deep voice grunted, but the grip around my torso never loosened.

"Where is he?"

The voice was exactly what I would have expected—rough, deep, impatient. It went perfectly with the mindless destruction that had been visited on T. C.'s little house.

It was not a reassuring thought.

I shook my head. "I don't know," I tried to say, but there was a fold of wool fabric over my mouth and my words were muffled.

I made a half-choked sound in the back of my throat and the iron grip eased slightly. "Kick me again, and you're dead," my captor rasped at my ear.

I shook my head again, trying to get the message across that I knew perfectly well I was outmuscled. "I don't know where T. C. is," I said, as clearly as I could manage. "I came looking for him."

"Huh." I couldn't tell what the wordless syllable meant. And then, after a pause, "You his girlfriend?"

I shook my head. It was hard to breathe when my own arms were being pressed against my rib cage like vise grips. I considered yelling as loudly as I could. There were houses close by, and people would likely be home at this time of day.

But most of T. C.'s neighbors were elderly. Even if they heard me, what could they do?

I could feel my whole frame shaking as I realized just how helpless I was.

"When'd you see him last?" the voice behind me demanded.

I had to force my brain to work. "Saturday," I said finally. "Saturday morning."

It seemed to take the stranger a long time to digest my replies. It didn't surprise me. Wrecking T. C.'s house hadn't been the work of a great intellect. It was wanton, childish, idiotic.

And so was his next move.

I felt him loosening one arm. But I didn't have time to try to take advantage of it before he hit me.

His fist caught me in the small of my back and knocked me headlong onto the floor. I gasped, more from surprise than pain, and tried to get to my hands and knees.

I didn't make it before the toe of his boot connected with my ribs. There was plenty of pain as well as shock this time, especially when he caught me a second time in the same place.

I gave up trying to fight back and followed my instincts to curl around myself and protect as much of my body as I could. My attacker paused, as though he'd been waiting for some signal of my surrender.

Then his feet rustled in the loose newspapers strewn across the floor. I wrapped my arms more tightly around myself, waiting for the next onslaught. But it didn't come.

Instead, the stranger pushed the screen door open. I wanted desperately to look up at him, but it would have meant rolling over and exposing too much of myself. I stayed where I was, trying to control the lurching of fear and pain in my gut as I listened to his parting words.

"Keep your mouth shut about this," he said, as he stepped through the screen door and out onto the porch.

He didn't add "Or else." He hardly had to. From my floor-level perspective, I could see the results of his rage everywhere. And I could feel them, too, in the throbbing of my ribs, my kidneys, my chin where it had scraped along the rough carpet.

I heard his footsteps moving away through the too-long grass. A minute later, the sound of an engine told me he must have parked his vehicle on the next street, out of sight.

My truck, however, was in clear view in T. C.'s driveway, colorfully emblazoned with "Henry's Towing" on both sides.

That meant that the man who'd just assaulted me knew who I was. And even if he wasn't an intellectual giant, it wouldn't take him much effort to find out where I lived.

The realization didn't make me feel any better as I slowly got off the floor and started to make my way home.

FOUR

"Geez, Rita. You look terrible. What happened?"

Davis Turnbull, my teenaged tenant and part-time employee, was sitting at the kitchen table eating ice cream when I finally limped in the door. Chili Dog was at his feet, gazing raptly at the nearly-empty ice cream container.

I'd already had to answer the same question when I'd stopped at Bruce's Pharmacy in uptown Athol to buy some bandages big enough to cover the nasty scrape on my chin. I kept a first-aid kit in the truck, but I'd used the last of my bandages when I'd cut myself a couple of weeks earlier. And fortunately, Bruce's was open until nine on Tuesday nights.

The young woman behind the counter had been a stranger to me, but that hadn't kept her from looking concerned. When she asked whether I was all right, I murmured something about having fallen in the dark. She was probably still back there, I thought, wondering whether she should have called some battered women's hotline.

And that was exactly what I was—a bruised and frightened woman. I'd stumbled into something I wanted no part of. And I had no idea, yet, what to do about it.

But I had to answer Davis's question somehow. "Slight disagreement with the wrecker," I muttered.

I wanted to tell him not to give the dog any ice cream because Chili was getting spoiled and lazy as it was. But I didn't want to stick around long enough for Davis to notice that I was walking as though I'd suddenly aged thirty years. I chose to ignore the sound of the ice cream carton hitting the floor and the skating noises it made as Chili stuck his broad muzzle inside and pushed it enthusiastically around. I wanted privacy, a hot bath, and a chance to think.

While the tub was filling, I took T. C.'s answering machine into my bedroom and plugged it in to a wall outlet next to my

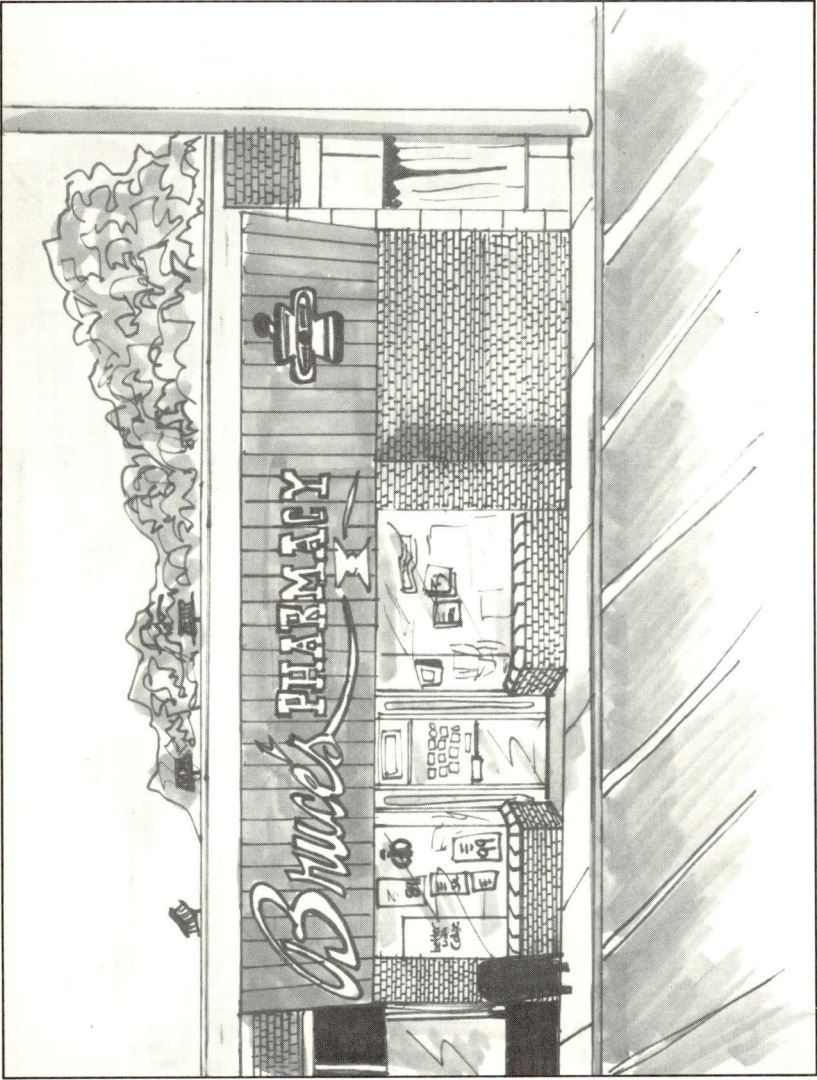

Bruce's Pharmacy

bed. The red light began flashing, indicating that there were messages.

The first was from the Athol Public Library. "The language tapes you requested are in," a pleasant female voice said, followed by a recorded voice dating the message on Saturday at a little before noon.

A receptionist from Athol Dental Associates had called on Saturday too, reminding T. C. of an appointment he'd made for Monday. The next message was from his parole officer, the man T. C. had nicknamed Mr. Magoo. He'd called on Sunday afternoon, requesting that T. C. check in as soon as he returned from Boston.

Evidently T. C. hadn't done it. There was a second, irritated call from Mr. Magoo on Monday morning. The young woman from Athol Dental Associates hadn't sounded any too pleased, either, when she'd let T. C. know he'd missed his scheduled appointment.

The parole officer had left another message on Monday afternoon, full of barely-veiled threats about what would happen to T. C. if he didn't call in soon. The message after that was mine, sounding only marginally less annoyed, inquiring whether T. C. had forgotten he was supposed to have dinner at my house.

Finally, Attorney Bill Oldach had called to discuss something about T. C.'s mother's estate. By this point it was startling to hear someone who *didn't* sound ready to wring T. C.'s neck.

"You're an original, Tom Carter," I said as I unplugged the answering machine. "I never knew anybody I could be so mad at and so worried about at the same time."

While I soaked in a hot bubble bath, I tried to figure out where that left me.

The man I'd been starting to fall in love with all over again had disappeared from my life as suddenly as he'd done more than thirty years earlier.

I'd just been threatened and pummeled by a stranger who obviously bore some kind of powerful grudge against T. C.

I didn't have any idea why.

And I wasn't completely convinced I'd seen the last of the man who'd kicked and punched me so hard I'd had to lower myself into the tub inch by painful inch.

The hot water felt wonderful. So did the knowledge that I wasn't alone in my house, that there was a dog who would bark and a teenaged boy who would call the police if anyone menaced me again tonight.

But that still didn't answer the question of what I was going to do next.

T. C. had been right when he'd said I never let go of things until I'd figured them out. And despite the fear that still clutched vaguely at me whenever I remembered the feeling of struggling against the dark folds of the coat that had blinded and half-suffocated me, my natural curiosity was starting to assert itself.

Where *had* T. C. disappeared to?

Did he know his house had been overturned? Was that why he'd left town? Or had the vandalism been the stranger's response to the discovery that T. C. was nowhere to be found?

One of the conditions of T. C.'s parole was that he be available whenever his parole officer chose to contact him. He was already in violation of that condition, already risking a return to prison.

Why? He'd hated jail—hated the confinement and boredom of it. I could think of very few reasons why he would chance being sent back.

Had some absolutely irresistible adventure come along to tempt him?

Or was he trying to escape something even worse than being locked up again?

The trouble with Tom Carter was that he was capable of virtually anything. Every explanation I came up with seemed more outlandish than the last. And then there were the possibilities I *wasn't* allowing myself to think about.

"Curiosity killed the cat, Rita," I told myself, as I leaned forward to pull the bathtub plug. "You've already gotten beaten up once. If T. C. couldn't be bothered confiding in you, why should you go out of your way trying to sort out his problems for him?"

The drain in my bathtub makes a desperate, suicidal noise. It's as though the water is being sucked out of the tub and straight into the center of the earth. As quickly as I could, to avoid being pulled down there with it, I got out onto the bath mat.

Because you're worried about him.

Because you care about him.

The answers I'd been avoiding popped up to meet me as I reached for a towel. I *did* care about Tom Carter. I couldn't help it.

And I couldn't help being concerned about him. Even the savviest tom cats run out of lives at some point. And the man who'd attacked me had sounded as though he didn't have an ounce of compassion in his body. If T. C. had gotten into something riskier than usual—

"I'm going to sleep on this," I announced to the steamy air in the bathroom. "And in the morning—assuming I'm not too sore to get out of bed—I'm probably going to decide that dropping this whole thing is the smartest thing I can do."

The visitor waiting on my doorstep the next morning changed my mind about that.

I recognized him immediately.

He had a round head and squinty eyes—Mr. Magoo personified. In case there'd been any doubt, the irritation in his voice perfectly matched the tone of the messages I'd heard on T. C.'s answering machine.

"Mrs. Magritte?" He sounded irritated with me, too. "I'm John MacGregor from the Department of Corrections. I'm here to speak with you about Thomas Carter."

Something about the little man instantly rubbed me the wrong way. He carried himself like a rooster, chest puffed up, head tilted back. His narrowed gray eyes looked as though he was prepared to disbelieve anything I might tell him. He seemed to be expecting an argument, and if he was always this abrupt and demanding, I thought, he probably got one more often than not.

"If you want to know where T. C. is," I said, "I don't have any idea."

Skepticism flooded his face. "Oh, come on, Mrs. Magritte," he said. "You've been keeping company with him ever since he came back to the area. Do you mean to tell me—"

I've always disliked that phrase. "I just *did* tell you," I said. "Look, I'm making coffee. Do you want some?"

He followed me into the kitchen, but I had the feeling it was because he wanted to keep an eye on me, not because he was taking me up on my offer. I noticed him peering down the hallway and into the living room.

There was the usual amount of clutter in the place—copies of the *Athol Daily News*, magazines I hadn't had a chance to read yet. Usually I didn't notice it. But Mr. Magoo obviously did.

It was like the old days, I thought. When I'd been a new bride, my mother had tended to drop in unexpectedly to see how my housekeeping skills were progressing. *Not fast enough*, had been her invariable, silent answer. It annoyed me to see this officious little man picking up right where she'd left off.

"You have family?" he asked, when he spotted Davis's Size 11 sneakers outside one of the bedroom doors.

"No."

"Whose shoes are those, then?"

"Not Tom Carter's, believe me."

I almost added that since they weren't, it really wasn't any of his business who they belonged to. My tone seemed to get that message across, and he looked even more distrustful as we entered the kitchen.

I'd bought myself a new bottle of Tia Maria recently at Stan's Liquor Mart in Athol. I'd poured a small glass of it before crawling into bed the night before, leaving the bottle sitting on the kitchen table. It was still there, and T. C.'s parole officer raised his eyebrows at it.

I had a sudden vision of how John MacGregor must see the world. To him, T. C. was an unreliable criminal, not to be trusted for a moment. And I could tell I was being tarred with exactly the same brush. I was obviously some kind of low-life, possibly even T. C.'s partner in crime.

The suspicion in the man's small eyes brought out every contrary instinct I had. "He's not under any of the beds or in any of the closets," I said, as I unplugged the coffee maker. "Do you want to check?"

"Being flippant is hardly appropriate under the circumstances, Mrs. Magritte." He frowned as Chili Dog clambered to his feet from his new doggy bed by the back door. "Is that a Rottweiler?" he asked.

"Mostly. He's a killer, of course. I trained him myself."

John MacGregor looked as though he wasn't certain I was joking. Chili shook his big head, setting his tags jangling, and ambled over to check out the stranger.

The parole officer backed quickly toward the hall. "Look, if you're not willing to tell me what you know about Tom Carter's whereabouts—"

I shook my head. "I *have* told you," I said. "I don't know anything."

"You went to his house—"

"How do you know that?" My voice was sharp.

He shook his head pityingly. "A neighbor saw your truck."

"Did you look inside the house?"

"Yes. It was a pig sty, as usual. He seemed to have been having some kind of wild party—which of course he's not supposed to be doing."

I shook my head in disbelief. Was John MacGregor stupid, or just willfully blind?

He seemed determined to see T. C. in as harsh a light as possible, and for the first time, I understood why T. C. had chafed so uncomfortably under this man's scrutiny. He was having the same effect on me. I wanted to do something outrageous, say something unpardonable, like a rebellious teenager determined to justify the world's bad opinion of me.

"Come on, Mrs. Magritte." He probably intended to sound cajoling, but his obvious unease at Chili Dog's closeness cut through his words like a cool breeze. "You're not helping him, you know."

It was at that moment that I decided I *would* help T. C., if only to prove this pompous little man wrong. I didn't like the idea that he'd been checking up on my movements. I didn't like the fact that he obviously thought I was lying. And it bothered me that he'd interpreted Chili's friendly, well-meaning approach as an attack.

Anyone who could be so wrong about Chili, and about me, was doomed to misunderstand T. C.'s free-spirited approach to life. Suddenly I found myself feeling protective about T. C., the man who was—unreliable or not—one of my oldest friends.

It didn't take long to get rid of Mr. Magoo. Between my tone of voice and my dog, he didn't stay long enough for the cup of coffee I'd already regretted offering him.

When he was gone, I grabbed a quick breakfast, tethered the dog in the yard, and made a list of the people I wanted to talk to in between the day's tow calls. It wasn't until I was climbing into the wrecker that it occurred to me my ribs still ached from yesterday's adventure. And I was heading west toward the center of Orange before I realized that the reason I was doing this, really, was that deep down I just wanted to see T. C. grinning at me again with that old outlaw glint in his sky-blue eyes.

FIVE

Like much of New England, the North Quabbin area boomed during the Industrial Revolution, leaving the landscape dotted with red brick factories. Some were still in use, others stood empty. But many had been converted to new purposes by enterprising developers who'd recognized that the spacious, centrally-located old buildings still had a great deal to offer.

North Quabbin Computer's office was in one of those. Occupying the first-floor corner of a structure right in the center of Orange, it looked out on the river through several tall windows along one wall. Someone had planted flowers in window boxes, and I could see their bright colors reflected in the smoothly flowing water below as I walked across the bridge from the municipal parking lot.

Inside, the place was a study in contrasts. A recent renovation had exposed the tall brick walls and wooden beams. A framed print of nineteenth-century Orange hung near the door. But everything else about the office was brand new, especially the modular furniture that divided the big room into several different areas and the computer components that seemed to be everywhere. There was a whole row of monitors lined up against the back wall on top of a set of shelves. They made me feel slightly uncomfortable, as though their blank gray screens were watching me.

As I closed the door behind me, a young man looked up from the computer where he was working and asked if he could help me.

"Is Casey Carter in?" I asked.

"Sure." He leaned over, looking toward the section of the room that fronted on the river. "Hey, Casey," he said. "You've got company."

In my green work clothes and heavy boots, I felt slightly out of place in the high-tech office. Davis had been bugging me lately about getting my business onto a computer, but I'd been resisting it, insisting it was just as easy for me to hand over each month's receipts to my accountant and let her sort it all out.

The sleek new computers in the North Quabbin Computer office, though, made me wonder if I was being hopelessly out of date. There were several slim laptop models along a counter top to my left, the kind Davis had just bought himself for college next year. As I looked around the place, I had to ask myself whether the idea of computerizing Henry's Towing bothered me because it just made me feel slow and old-fashioned, several steps out of sync with the times.

"You either plunge in or you get left behind, Rita." I could almost hear T. C.'s deep voice saying the words. Was he right? I wondered. Had I chosen to be too safe, stayed too close to home?

"Rita. What can I do for you?"

For an instant I thought it *was* T. C. Then I blinked and realized the voice I'd heard belonged to his younger brother, who was approaching me from the river side of the room.

The two of them had always sounded similar. They looked similar, too, except that Casey's graying hair was neatly trimmed, his white shirt impeccable, his smile pleasant and businesslike, nothing at all like his brother's renegade grin.

"Don't tell me you've decided to enter the electronic age at last." He shook my hand and ushered me ahead of him into a corner that seemed to function as both workbench and office. "We can still get Henry's Towing on-line before the millennium, if we hurry."

I shook my head. Casey, like me, had stayed close to home for most of his life. In another sense, though, he'd plunged ahead with the rest of the world, choosing a career in computers when the field was still new. In his late forties now, he was a successful consultant, whose polished manner told me I would be in capable hands if I ever did steer my way onto the electronic superhighway.

But that wasn't why I'd come. "It's about T. C.," I said and watched Casey's professional smile dim. "I'm worried about him, Casey."

The two Carter boys had been close as children. But T. C.'s teenage shenanigans had seemed to embarrass his younger brother. Casey had struggled to get out from under his sibling's wild reputation. From the look on his face now, the struggle wasn't over.

"You're not the first person to come and ask me about this," he said slowly.

"Don't tell me," I said. "A little guy with round glasses, right?"

He nodded. "Looked like Mr. Magoo," he said.

"That's what T. C. says, too."

The coincidence obviously didn't please him. "Look, Rita, you know T. C. and I haven't had much to do with each other since he got back to town," he said.

"I know. I just thought—"

What *had* I thought? I'd hoped that by asking questions, perhaps stirring things up a little, I might be able to shed some light on T. C.'s mysterious disappearance. It was a technique that had worked for me before.

"I thought you might know if he was in some kind of trouble," I finished.

Casey's short laugh didn't sound amused. "When was T. C. ever *not* in trouble?" he asked.

It was a good question. I hadn't come up with a good answer for it before Casey continued, "I appreciate that you're being loyal to my brother. Lord knows he needs all the friends he can get. But I learned a long time ago that getting too close to him is just setting myself up for a lot of grief. He doesn't know how to put down roots, Rita. He can't even stay in one place when he knows perfectly well the alternative is going back to prison. I've dealt with that by just not letting him play a big role in my life. So I don't know anything about where he is or what he thinks he's up to now—and frankly, that's the way I prefer it."

I looked closely at him. He seemed so sincere, so clear about his own thinking. And yet there was a sound somewhere in his voice that made me think he wasn't quite as indifferent as he seemed.

"That seems sad," I said. "Neither of you has much family, except for each other."

Something flashed in his blue eyes, so similar to and yet so different from T. C.'s. It was a warning, I thought. *Don't pity me* was the clear message in his face.

"I have my wife and kids," he said. "I have a granddaughter I adore and another one on the way. I have a home and a career I worked hard for and a connection to this community I value very much. What has T. C. done in his life that compares with any of that?"

Nothing, I thought, as I left the North Quabbin Computer office. Not unless you counted a thousand unlikely adventures and a laugh that could lighten a woman's heart.

And mine wasn't only heart he affected that way. I knew, from T. C.'s stray comments, that his niece and grandniece, the daughter and granddaughter Casey had just mentioned, were as fond of T. C. as I was.

Maybe you had to be a woman to appreciate that seductively irreverent laugh, I thought. Or maybe you just had to have a hidden streak of rebelliousness yourself.

And it was clear that I did—because it was beginning to occur to me that the more I listened to people putting T. C. down, the more determined I was becoming to find him if I could.

I was about to pull out of the parking lot when a call came in on my mobile phone. The driver had broken down on Route 2A just on the other side of Orange and was calling from the pay phone outside the Walmart store. Could I tow him to Greenfield right away?

I could, although I took a couple of minutes to stop at the Village Grille, just up South Main Street from the computer office, to get a couple of their homemade muffins to go. My annoyance at Mr. Magoo had driven the thought of breakfast out of my head, and my stomach was rumbling.

It was nearly noon by the time I got back. I headed straight to the next name on my list—Warner Cable on New Athol Road.

The cable company had moved from downtown Athol to a brand-new building a couple of years earlier. It was the opposite of the computer office: everything at Warner Cable was very muted and modern, with a pleasant reception area painted in a pale shade of pink.

But here, too, I felt somewhat out of place. Next to the pair of clean white company vans in the parking lot, my wrecker looked oversized and clumsy. And my work clothes would have been more at home in the shop out back than in the neat public area I'd stepped into.

Where *did* I belong? I found myself wondering as I walked up to the counter. And why was I spending so much time worrying about it all of a sudden?

I knew the answer to that one. T. C.'s reappearance in my life had shaken me out of my everyday routine, making me question things I'd taken for granted for a lot of years.

And no matter how T. C. might infuriate me at times, I felt at home when I was with him. That was why I was on this unlikely chase, even though I knew perfectly well there might turn out to be nothing but a wild goose at the end of it.

The woman who came to the counter to meet me looked concerned when I told her I wanted to speak to one of their technicians.

"If it's a complaint, we handle those through the office," she said. "We want to make sure our customers are happy, so—"

"It's nothing like that," I assured her. "In fact, I'm a happy customer myself. I just happened to notice one of your trucks in front of a friend's house the other day. My friend asked me to keep an eye on his place while he's away, and there was some minor damage done over the past few days. I was hoping your driver might have noticed something that would give me an idea who'd done it."

The look of concern didn't lift from her face. "Have you called the police?" she asked.

"Of course." It was amazing, I thought, how easily I could lie when I set my mind to it. In fact, I had no intention of calling the police, not until I knew which side of this mess T. C. happened to be on.

"This is just for my own peace of mind," I said. "I have a pretty good idea who's responsible. I'm just seeing if I can confirm it."

"Well, in that case—" She consulted a list on one of the nearby desks. "What's your friend's address?"

Most of the technicians were at lunch, she told me, once she'd looked up the service record for T. C.'s house. But I was in luck. If I didn't mind waiting for a few minutes, the man who'd installed T. C.'s cable was due back at the office shortly.

It took half an hour, by which time a tow call had come in for me. A farm truck had gotten stuck up at Maple Valley Farm, and after wrestling with it all morning, they'd decided they needed professional help to pull it loose.

I told them I'd be there as soon as I could manage. By the time T. C.'s cable technician arrived, I was starting to feel impatient, and asking myself how much paying work I could afford to delay while I tried to track down Tom Carter.

Things got delayed a little more while I tried to bring the technician around to the point. He was a garrulous young man in his twenties, willing and eager to tell me all about his own working day.

"I'd have been back here sooner," he said, as I followed him into the back of the building, "but I had to make an extra stop before lunch. There's an older couple downtown in Athol who wanted a new cable box hooked up before their relatives come to visit or something like that. We got talking—turns out she's from Nashua, same as me. Only she left a long time before me, naturally.

"Anyway, she wrote a book called *Listen, My Dears* about growing up in Nashua. Her name's Mrs. Haven—Grandma Haven. So we had to swap memories about Nashua for a while. I like talking to my customers—you meet a lot of nice people that way."

I told him it was not-so-nice people I was looking for. "Did you happen to see anything unusual when you were doing that installation out on White Pond Road on Monday?" I asked.

He thought for a moment, then unrolled the grinder he'd pulled out of a Subway bag, along with a soda. I thought about him chatting happily with Grandma Haven and then stopping to get his lunch at the Subway on Athol's Main Street while I was waiting to get the wrecker back on the road toward my own customers.

Patience, Rita, I told myself. *You already know this amateur detective business isn't easy.*

At first it looked as though Warner Cable was going to prove to be a dead end. The young technician thought about my question, then shook his head.

"It was a pretty routine job," he said. "No problems or anything. The customer wasn't home, but we just had to run a new line from the street. The inside work was already done."

"Did you notice anything out of the ordinary around the house?"

Again the technician shook his head. "Looked normal to me," he said. "Nice little place, right on the water like that. I was saying to the gardener—"

"Hold on." I looked more sharply at him. "The who?"

"The gardener. You know, the guy who mows the lawn."

"The lawn wasn't mowed this week."

"I know. He couldn't get the mower started. But we chatted a bit, you know, just passing the time of day while I was hooking up the cable. I said I'd always liked looking at the water, and he said, yeah, he grew up on the south shore of Boston, and he liked the water, too."

"What did he look like?"

"Oh, taller than me, maybe five-nine or ten. Muscular guy, kind of heavy. Dark curly hair. He had sunglasses on, so I couldn't see the color of his eyes."

"Was he wearing a coat?"

For the first time it seemed to occur to him to wonder why I was asking about this. "Yeah," he said slowly. "He had a Red Sox jacket on. You know, the wool kind."

I knew the kind.

I also knew that the fabric that had half-smothered me on Tuesday evening had smelled like wool—well-worn wool, mixed with sweat and aftershave.

"Did you see anything else? A car or anything? Or did he say—"

"That was all we talked about—the water, and that he couldn't get the lawn mower going." He frowned. I had a feeling his garrulousness had just run out. "Look, what's this about, anyway? You said he was some friend of yours?"

"The owner of the house is a friend," I said. "I was just trying to answer a question. Thanks for your help."

I'd answered a question, all right. I had at least a partial description of the man who'd almost certainly trashed T. C.'s house and beaten me up. Dark, with curly hair, a heavy build. It wasn't the whole answer, but it was a lot more than I'd had before.

Despite the warmth of the June day, I shivered slightly as I climbed into the wrecker and headed for North Orange and Maple Valley Farm. I could still hear that rough voice saying *Keep your mouth shut about this* as I lay in a frightened heap on the floor at his feet.

Since I obviously didn't have the sense to follow his advice, I was glad I had some idea what he looked like. At least now, I thought, I would know who I was watching out for.

SIX

"You're looking for *what*?"

I've never figured out how teenagers learn to pack so much sarcasm into a simple phrase. Davis Turnbull was a master at it.

"Why restrict it to the Greater Boston area?" he went on, pushing his dark red hair out of his eyes as he looked at me from behind one of the big computer screens in the *Athol Daily News* office. "Why not just do a search for every guy named Rick in the western hemisphere?"

"Are you done?" I asked him. "Or would you like to roll your eyes at me some more before I finish what I was going to say?"

He *did* roll his eyes. "You said you were looking for a guy named Rick," he pointed out. "And that he probably—"

"I know what I said. What you didn't let me add was that this guy named Rick was T. C.'s codefendant last year. Or at least, they were arrested at the same time. I want to know more about Rick—starting with a last name."

"You're still looking for T. C., huh."

It wasn't a question, so I didn't answer it. Davis didn't like T. C. Neither did Chili Dog. The single time I'd invited T. C. over to my house, the pair of them had sat and glared at him the whole time. T. C. commented afterward that he had the feeling they were trying to work themselves up to ask him what his intentions toward me were.

"I could have told them that," I'd said, laughing. "Thoroughly dishonorable."

"Yeah, but young guys don't like to think old guys know anything about that stuff," he'd replied. "And dogs—well, dogs just don't like stray tom cats."

Davis still didn't look happy about my request for information about T. C.'s old friend Rick. But he agreed to dig up whatever he could through the newspaper's computer files. The

Daily News was fully in step with the twentieth century—or perhaps the twenty-first, I thought whenever I looked at the big monitors in the room where Davis was working. For a small-town paper, it was impressively well-connected to the rest of the world.

In addition to acting as my weekend dispatcher, Davis was a full-time reporter for the newspaper. They seemed to recognize his talent, because they'd already told him he could work for them during the summers even after he started at Columbia University next fall.

"I'll meet you at the bookstore in about an hour," Davis said. "Tina and I are going to dinner at Eddie's. I'm picking her up after work."

"What's the occasion?" Like Davis, his girlfriend Tina was working at two jobs to save as much money as she could for college. I hadn't seen either of them spend a frivolous penny in months. The news that they were going out to Eddie's Italian Restaurant, a local favorite on South Street, surprised me.

Davis actually blushed under his overhanging curtain of hair. "It's our anniversary," he said. "Two years since our first date."

I stared at him. He worked so hard to seem like a cynical young journalist-about-town that I frequently forgot he had a softer side.

"Good for you, Davis," I said. "You deserve a treat."

He looked suspiciously at me. "You're making fun of us," he said.

"I'm not. It's just—"

I shook my head. No doubt my parents had looked at me and T. C. when we'd been keeping company in high school, and thought it might be better if the transition to adulthood happened more slowly. Had they marvelled, as I was marvelling now, at how quickly young lovers assumed all the trappings of grown-up love—the anniversaries, the social calendar, the shared plans for a future they were so confident they would share?

Young love was so fragile, I thought. And everyone knew that except young lovers themselves.

I remembered how sure I'd been at seventeen that Tom Carter was my destiny, my soul-mate. Instead, I'd married steady, easy-going Henry Magritte and ended up in middle age still in my home town, as a tow-truck driver, of all things.

Davis was certain that he was headed for a brilliant career in journalism, with Tina at his side. But who knew what twists and detours would present themselves in his own young life?

"I'm just feeling my age," I told him and left it at that.

The weather had stayed gray, and despite the approach of the longest day of the year in just a couple of weeks, the evening was already darkening when I walked into the Hobbit Doorway just before seven.

The store was as cheerful as ever, though, thanks to the eye-catching displays of books, jewelry, and gifts that filled every corner of it. There were displays of odds and ends—pens and pencils, games, bookmarks—lining the length of the counter. Draped above on a hanging rack was a red and white coverlet with North Quabbin scenes woven into it, making a bright banner of the local history and landscape.

"We're just about to close." I heard Tina's voice, then saw her blond head appearing around a rack of cards near the back of the store.

"Oh, hi, Rita," she said when she spotted me. "I'm just feeding the cat. I'll be right there."

The store's owner had acquired a cat some time before, a lanky black and white male named Pennywise who ranged around the place as though it was his own private stretch of veldt. I'd seen him sleeping contentedly in various corners when I'd visited the store, and I'd also seen him in more kittenish moods, racing from room to room of the old house on his long beanstalk legs.

He apparently had work to do, too—occasionally there had been cat-related books on display near the front door, with a sign stating that the bookstore cat personally recommended them. But he clearly didn't work for free, given the way he was demanding his dinner.

His loud scratchy voice carried all the way to the front of the store. "Hold on, would you?" Tina was replying. "Anybody would think you hadn't eaten in a week."

I walked back to meet her, in time to see Pennywise attacking his dinner in the small bathroom where his dish and litter box lived. "Sorry, Rita," Tina said, as she stepped out of the little room. "Is there something I can help you find before I close up?"

After several months of working at it, I'd finally gotten her to stop calling me "Mrs. Magritte." She was still extraordinarily polite to me, though. Davis didn't get along with either of his parents—that was how he'd ended up staying with me. Sometimes I thought Tina saw me as a surrogate mother-in-law on whom she wanted to make a good impression.

I explained why I was there and stood aside while she finished closing up the store. I bought a copy of the Athol paper and read it on the porch while I waited. The day's news was the usual mix of local and international, routine and bizarre.

The Orange selectboard had deferred a decision about a possible expansion of the airport. A fire had gutted an old warehouse in Athol. And a woman had given birth aboard a commercial airplane bound for L. A., leading to speculation that airlines might place restrictions on women traveling in their final month of pregnancy.

"Bet that's one adventure T. C. never had to deal with," I thought as I folded up the paper. From military cargoes to wilderness hikers to hunting parties, T. C.'s passengers over his long and checkered career had had one thing in common: like T. C. himself, they were far outside the domestic realm.

Davis shambled up the front walk as his girlfriend was bringing in the last of the display items from the porch. His legs were as long and skinny as the black and white cat's, I thought. He always looked disjointed, barely bolted together.

But his green eyes were focused and sharp as he handed me a sheaf of computer paper. "There's your boy," he said. "Richard Sayles, lives in Somerville. Turns out he was in Vietnam with T. C."

"Good job," I said. I'd already known T. C. and his friend Rick had met when they were both in the Air Force. But I hadn't known Rick's last name or where he lived.

And now that I did, maybe I could find out whether he had dark curly hair and a voice like a knife blade that needed sharpening.

"I copied off everything I could find about the arrests and convictions." Davis nodded at the pages he'd given me. "There's not much. But the Boston papers had a little more detail than we gave it at the *Daily News*." He frowned, and added, "You know, Rita, even if you do manage to find T. C.—"

I could tell what was coming, and I didn't want to hear it. It was one thing for me, at fifty, to feel wise and philosophical about Davis's future. It was something very different to have Davis, who was barely nineteen, offering advice about my own affairs of the heart.

I folded the pages he'd given me and stepped off the porch. "Thanks for your help, Davis," I said. "I take back some of the hostile things I've been saying about computers. Have a great time at Eddie's, both of you."

I didn't want to tell him that I had no clear idea what I was going to do if and when I found T. C.

And I didn't tell him, either, that I'd slipped Tina a twenty-dollar bill while I was waiting, in honor of their "anniversary" and all the ardor and ambiguity of first love.

On Thursday, the gray clouds opened up. Rainy weather—especially after a dry spell—means tow truck drivers will be busy pulling people out of ditches they've skidded into. Thursday was no exception. In spite of the sudden flood of work, though, I did manage to find time for a lunch break when my son Mike called and murmured the three words I can never resist.

"Canadian meat pie," he said. "Meet you at Woody's?"

Woody's Main Street Diner in Athol is one of my favorite places to eat. And I have a special fondness for the Thursday lunch special. Besides, Mike worked hard himself at his one-man garage. If he could make time for lunch with his mother, I wasn't about to turn him down.

"Hannah's worried you're not taking this baby shower thing seriously," he said as we slid onto a pair of stools at the diner's busy counter just after one-thirty.

Mike is like me: he prefers the direct approach. I stirred sugar into the coffee that Ann, the waitress, had set in front of me and looked up at the bakery case full of homemade pies and puddings that Woody miraculously managed to replenish five days a week.

"I've been busy," I said. "And Hannah worries too much."

"I know that, Mom. I'm just passing on what she's been telling me. I can't help it if she calls to bend my ear about this stuff, can I?"

We paused long enough to place our two orders of meat pie and to say hello to Patty, the other waitress, who was busy handing takeout orders past us to customers who'd just arrived. At the grill, Woody was turning out barbecued chicken breasts, one of the day's specials. At the other end of the diner, Brad was serving meat pie and fried food orders.

"Everything always works so smoothly here," I said, a little resentfully. "Why isn't my life this organized?"

Mike grinned at me. "If Hannah had her way, it would be," he said.

"I know." I watched Brad hand a takeout order to Patty, who passed it along to a waiting customer with one hand while collecting the woman's money with the other. "Maybe I just need a good staff like Woody's got."

Woody's Main Street Diner

"Sure." Mike's grin broadened. "You could have one flunky to walk to dog, one to bake goodies when Hannah needs them, one to remind you to go to the bank—"

"Oh, shoot." I'd meant to visit the bank earlier in the day, but the sudden spate of business had driven it right out of my mind. "I'm glad you mentioned that."

You managed to remember to call T. C.'s friend Rick Sayles, didn't you? my conscience pointed out. Of course, it hadn't led anywhere. Rick Sayles' phone was disconnected, the computerized voice told me. But I *had* remembered to do it, even though I'd forgotten all about the bank.

"See? Now, if you just had somebody to ride herd on every little detail for you—" Mike's smile faded. "Or a partner, maybe."

"I'm not in the market for a partner," I said firmly. I knew he was thinking about T. C.

"Hannah thinks you are. It's driving her nuts. She can't decide whether to be ecstatic that you might be doing something normal for once in your life or furious because you're hanging around with the town bad boy."

"Hanging around is *all* I'm doing at this stage." I moved my elbows off the counter to make room for my dinner. "But if I *was* doing more—what would you think about it, Mike?"

Mike is like Henry, too—deliberate, thoughtful, and open-minded. I could overlook Davis's disapproval and Hannah's outrage, but I was more inclined to take Mike's opinion seriously.

His expression told me he wasn't any happier about T. C. than anyone else I knew.

"I just think you deserve to be happy, Mom," he said. "Your track record's good so far. I wouldn't want to see that change."

Meaning, I thought, that Mike's father and I had had a good marriage—compatible, trusting, built on mutual love and respect. What I'd had with Henry had been solid and real.

Clearly, Mike didn't see a romance with T. C. as leading to anything so satisfying.

Was I a fool even to think of reaching for the lost dreams I thought I'd seen in Tom Carter's blue eyes? Was all of that nothing but fantasy, after all? The thought of it wasn't enough to blight my appetite, but our lunch was quieter than usual as we both chewed over the questions.

SEVEN

At two o'clock, well-fed but no nearer to an answer, I waved good-bye to Mike and went across the street to the Orange Savings Bank. I had to make a payment on my truck insurance, and I wanted to transfer some money into my checking account first.

I paused on the way past Emily's Needleworks, a new sewing and craft store right next to the bookstore on Main Street. The rain had momentarily stopped, and I could see my reflection in the big plate glass window.

I shook my head at the sight. Nothing about me looked in the least romantic, from my well-padded frame to the skeptical glint in my brown eyes. My dark auburn hair was starting to go gray in a determined way, which I wasn't bothering to color over. It was cut more in favor of practicality than style. And my green work clothes were anything but flattering.

But somewhere inside me the teenaged heart that had once been swept away by Tom Carter's charm was still beating away. "You'd better get a grip on yourself, Rita," I muttered, "or you're going to find yourself running away to join the circus or something."

The mundane activity of banking seemed like a good way to remind myself of the realities of my everyday life. But even in the bank I couldn't escape my thoughts of T. C.

What reminded me was the sight of his niece Angela waiting in the reception area. The Athol branch of Orange Savings Bank is smaller than the main office in Orange, with the teller windows and the service area and the managers' offices all in clear view of one another. Angela Carter was sitting in one of the chairs near the line for the tellers, obviously waiting to speak to someone at one of the service desks.

Her little girl—Casey's granddaughter, T. C.'s great-niece—was with her. The Orange Savings Bank, in its wisdom, provided a box of toys for its customers' children, something I wished banks had thought of in the days when I'd had two bored kids waiting with me in line.

Angela's little girl was about eighteen months old. She'd gone immediately for the brightly-colored plastic blocks in the toy box and was happily arranging and rearranging them on the carpeted floor.

Angela was watching her do it, but she looked up when I spoke to her.

"Rita!" She gave me a tired smile. She was an attractive young woman, with jet-black hair like T. C.'s and Casey's had once been. I could easily understand why she looked tired. Like Hannah, she was several months pregnant. And with a toddler to look after already, Angela had more than enough to keep her busy.

"How're you doing, Angie? And how about you, sweetie?" I squatted down and reached out a forefinger to the baby, who promptly latched onto it.

"Oh, I'm okay. Just dragging a bit in this dreary weather. And—" Her expression as she looked around was almost conspiratorial. "I guess I can say this to you, Rita, although nobody else seems to want to hear it. But I'm worried about T. C. Have you heard anything at all from him?"

We might as well be conspirators, I thought, recalling that even my broad-minded son Mike had had nothing good to say about Tom Carter.

I admitted to Angie that I hadn't heard a thing, but that I was doing a little digging around to see whether I could turn up any ideas about where her uncle had gone.

Her tired face brightened a little. "That's good," she said. "I'm glad *somebody* cares where he's gotten to. Somebody besides that awful little parole man, I mean."

The baby picked up one of the plastic blocks and heaved it toward me. I caught it and handed it back.

"I really thought he was going to stick around this time," Angie went on. "I know that sounds like wishful thinking, but— well, he's always been my favorite uncle. It was great when I was a kid, having this dashing, handsome pilot visiting, you know?"

"I know," I said with feeling.

"I was hoping he was getting old enough that he would stop chasing around all over the place."

To Angela, in her all-knowing twenties, fifty probably seemed ancient. I decided not to tell her I'd just been communing with my inner adolescent a few minutes earlier.

"But this—disappearing this way—" Angela's face dimmed again. "It probably means he'll have to go back to jail, doesn't it? I mean, he wasn't supposed to leave the area, and now—"

She shook her dark head. "I can't understand it. He *hated* jail. I visited him there a couple of times, and all he could talk about was how much he wanted to get out."

"I know." The same point had been bothering me, making me think that wherever T. C. was, it seemed unlikely he'd gone there voluntarily. "Any kind of restriction makes him crazy. You should have seen him as a high-school student."

She smiled wanly and reached down to keep her daughter from trying to absorb one of the colored blocks through her mouth. "I can imagine," she said. "Or as a married man."

Good point, Rita, I told myself. *T. C.'s not the kind to settle down, as though you needed to be reminded of that.*

"How long exactly was he married?" I asked casually.

"A year and a half," Angela said. "He told me there were two kinds of language barriers—the one between English and Russian, and the one over what each of them meant when they talked about 'commitment.' T. C. thought it meant not sleeping with anybody else, but his wife had ideas about them actually making a home together and stuff."

"I didn't know she was Russian," I said.

Angie nodded. "She was the daughter of some scientist who was working on a research project in northern Canada. T. C. flew her and her father in and out of the wilderness a bunch of times. I guess it was one of those romantic things that couldn't survive in the everyday world."

I felt the sting of the comment. But if it showed in my face, Angie didn't seem to notice. "He acts like it didn't mean anything to him," she continued. "But I think it did, especially that he never got to see his daughter again."

"His daughter." I was so astonished I couldn't even make a question out of it.

Once again, Angie didn't seem to notice my reaction. "Yeah," she said. "It was sad, wasn't it?"

T. C. hadn't said a word to me about a daughter—not unless you counted his unexpectedly wistful comment about how it would be nice to have grandchildren. He'd been vague on the whole subject of his marriage, in fact.

It was hard to picture him as father, even an absentee one. I knew this revelation had nothing to do with my current quest to find out where he'd disappeared and why. But I couldn't squelch my own curiosity about this new facet of the man I knew so well in some ways and not at all in others.

"Where exactly does his daughter live now?" I asked.

"I have no idea how you pronounce the name of it." Angie laughed. "Heck, she probably can't pronounce 'Athol, Massachusetts,' either. I guess she doesn't speak any English at all."

So T. C.'s wife must have taken the baby back to Russia with her after the divorce. I thought fast, trying to piece the whole picture together.

"And she'd be—how old now?" I asked, as casually as I could. I didn't want to let Angie know that I was completely in the dark about T. C.'s marriage and child. Angie was touchingly loyal to her tomcat uncle. If she thought she was betraying his confidences—

Her sharp look told me she was beginning to catch on to the way I was fishing for information. "In her twenties," she said slowly. "Didn't T. C. tell you that?"

"Well—"

I was spared having to come up with a white lie by the approach of a woman from the service area, inviting Angela to come and have a seat. She got to her feet slowly, easing the obvious strain on her lower back.

"I'll tell you one thing," she said. "That woman who had her baby on the airplane in L. A. must have been out of her mind to be trying to go halfway around the world in this condition. If I could manage it, I wouldn't even come downtown again until after this one arrives."

Stay home. Stay safe. Don't rock the boat. The message kept coming at me from too many sources to ignore.

And all I had to counter those sensible warnings was the memory of T. C.'s laughing blue eyes, and the feeling of lifting off into a glowing sunset sky with him at the controls of a two-seater plane.

Was I a fool? Or a middle-aged dreamer? Or just too stubborn to give up on a quest once I'd started one?

"All of the above," I said to myself as I left the Orange Savings Bank and went back out into the rain that was steadily beating down again.

I left the wrecker where it was and walked up the street to Cornerstone Insurance to make my payment. Thursday is payday for a lot of people in Athol, and consequently, most of the area businesses are busiest on that day. Cornerstone was no exception, and I had to stand in line behind someone picking up a set of new license plates and someone else asking for advice about a health insurance statement.

I didn't mind waiting. My beeper was silent for the moment, and at least I was in out of the rain. Besides, I'd gotten plenty of good advice myself at the insurance agency.

It occurred to me while I waited, in fact, that in some sense they'd been like the staff of helpers Mike had jokingly told me I needed. Cornerstone's courier had been available to take my truck renewal to the Motor Vehicle Registry whenever I'd found myself squeezed for time. And there'd been plenty of days—

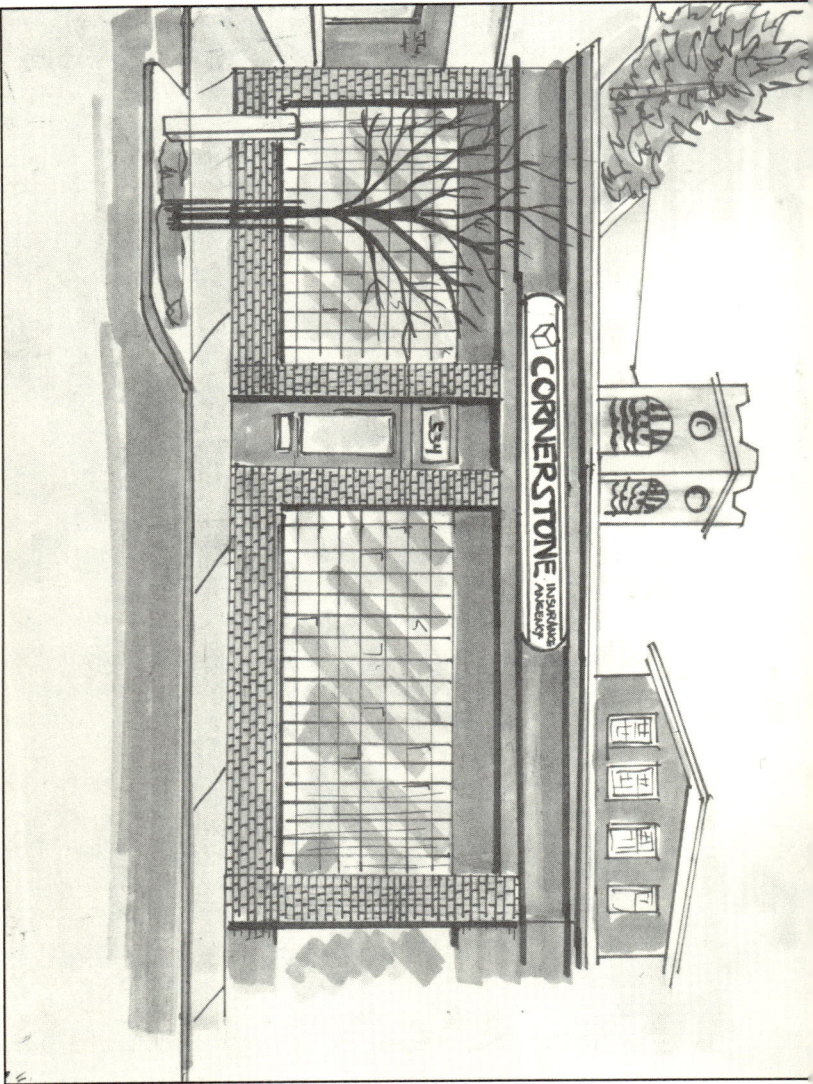

Cornerstone Insurance

like this one—when it had been very handy to be able to make a last-minute payment here.

Besides, I didn't mind the few extra minutes to stand and think.

So far I'd learned very little of what I wanted to know. I'd discovered that someone disliked T. C. enough to overturn his house and threaten his acquaintances. I'd confirmed that T. C.'s parole officer was an officious little man with no sympathy whatsoever for his charge.

I'd learned that T. C. not only had an estranged wife but a daughter he hadn't seen in more than twenty years. And I'd found that among his other family, only his niece seemed worried about where he was or what might be happening to him.

I'd discovered the last name and home town of T. C.'s old war buddy, who'd been arrested with him the past year.

As evidence went, it didn't amount to much.

And that was why, once I'd made my insurance payment, I decided to go next door to the Athol Public Library. I wanted to find out what the language tapes were that T. C. had requested, the ones they'd called to tell him were in.

They couldn't tell me, the woman at the desk said politely. People's library records were confidential, by law.

Faced with one dead end, I tried the only other lead I could think of: looking up T. C.'s friend Rick Sayles' street address in the library's Boston telephone book.

I knew I should be spending at least part of tomorrow baking the elegant goodies Hannah was expecting for her baby shower. But try as I might, I couldn't push that to the top of my list yet. Rick Sayles' phone was disconnected, but I might learn something from visiting the place where he could very well still be living.

I would start baking after I got back from the city, I promised myself. And with luck, by that time I would have tracked down Rick Sayles and come a little closer to solving the mystery of where my once and future beau had disappeared.

Something happened during the night that made it seem even more urgent to do that.

The rain kept up, and at eleven o'clock, I got a call from Davis. "Guy's van popped a tire," he said. "He managed to pull it over in New Salem. It's parked in the lawyer's lot now—you know, Ann Clukay-Whittier, right on Route 202. He hasn't got a spare, and he thinks he bent the rim. Oh, and he says he absolutely has to get back to Boston tonight. You want to do it?"

Three things prompted me to say yes. One was the fact that the customer had a road service account that would compensate me more than adequately for the nuisance of driving into the city in the pouring rain with a van in tow.

The second was that driving into the city in the pouring rain was a whole lot easier when there wasn't any traffic.

And, finally, it occurred to me that since I'd been planning to go into Boston anyway to find Rick Sayles, I might as well make the trip now, find a motel room for the night, and get an early start on my search in the morning.

The next phone call made me think I'd made the right decision.

It came in just as I finished hooking up the van. Sodden and chilled, the driver and I were climbing into the cab as the cell phone rang.

"Well, if it isn't Mrs. Henry's Towing." I shivered at the sound of the voice, and it had nothing to do with how wet I'd gotten rigging my customer's vehicle up to my truck. The last time I'd heard that voice, I'd had a wool jacket over my head and my arms pinned helplessly to my sides.

"Going into Boston, huh?" the caller said.

"Who told you that?" My voice was sharp with anxiety.

"The kid at your house. I know where you live, you know. I know lots of things about you. The only important thing I don't know about you is why you won't tell me where Tom Carter is."

"I *did* tell you. I don't know where he is."

"The hell you don't."

"Look, you're wasting your time," I said. "I'm just—"

"I know what you're doing. And when you come back, I'll be here waiting for you. Just remember that."

Suddenly, staying overnight in Boston seemed like a very good idea. I swallowed as I listened to the dial tone at my ear. Despite the street lights illuminating the center of New Salem, the rainy night around me felt very dark and very threatening as the echoes of that raspy, malicious voice lingered in my ears.

I called Davis immediately and told him to be extra careful locking up and setting the alarm before he went to bed. I cut off his protests and hoped my instincts were right: that T. C.'s antagonist was only interested in harassing people who might lead him to T. C. himself. I was virtually certain Davis didn't fall into that category.

I was just as certain I didn't want to run into the stranger again, especially not on this dark, wet night. Shrugging off my customer's questions about the phone call, I turned the windshield wipers on and started driving east.

EIGHT

Parts of Somerville, Massachusetts, are very pleasant, with well-kept two- and three-story houses lining the city streets.

Other parts aren't.

Rick Sayles lived in one of the other parts. All the best routes around metropolitan Boston prohibit commercial vehicles like my truck, so I took the subway and then a bus to get there. Besides, I knew the parking situation in the city, and I didn't want to spend half the morning trying to find a legal parking space the wrecker would fit into.

Instead, I spent it walking through the rain to the very end of a street far from any known bus route.

I'd spent a comfortable night in a motel near the end of the subway line in Cambridge. I keep a little overnight bag under the seat of the wrecker for emergencies, and I'd watched closely as I'd driven to the motel from my customer's house in Arlington. I was certain no one had followed me, so for the moment, I was dry, reasonably well provided for, and safe from the raspy-voiced man.

The next morning, however, was another matter.

When I finally did locate Rick Sayles' street, I couldn't find the right house. The street numbers were misleading, and I had to ask two neighbors for help. The first one I tried spoke only Spanish, and my lame pantomiming of the few things I knew about Rick Sayles—that he was a pilot, that he'd been arrested a year ago—just puzzled her. The second woman didn't know his name, but she nodded when I mentioned the bar fight. "Oh, sure, him," she said. "He's in that building right across the street."

"Is he a heavy guy, with dark curly hair?" I asked. "Sometimes wears a Red Sox jacket?"

She shook her head. "No," she said. "He's got gray hair, really gray, and a moustache."

There were names in only three of the eight slots on the mailboxes in the building across the street. Rick Sayles' wasn't one of them. I had to ask another neighbor before I found out he lived on the top floor in the back.

And then he wasn't home.

I knocked and waited several times, hoping perhaps he was just sleeping. Finally, though, I had to admit defeat.

I considered sitting down on the steps and waiting. The idea didn't appeal to me. A couple of apartment doors had opened and closed again as I'd climbed the stairs, and I hadn't been reassured by the glimpses I'd caught of Rick Sayles' fellow-tenants. He lived in a hard neighborhood. And after tangling with one bully already during the week, I wasn't looking for any more close encounters of the physical kind.

But I didn't want to walk all the way back to the bus stop, either. It had taken me more than an hour to get there in the first place.

There'd been a neighborhood bar between the apartment building and the bus stop, I recalled. It was very possible that it had been the scene of the infamous bar fight that had landed T. C. in this latest round of trouble. Maybe if I went in and ordered a sandwich or something—

I was still trying to decide whether I'd more likely be laughed out of the place or thrown out when I heard footsteps on the wooden stairs below me. A woman was approaching the top floor.

"What do you want?" She didn't look pleased at the sight of me on the landing.

I told her I was looking for Rick Sayles, which didn't seem to make her any happier. "He's not here," she said.

"Do you know when he'll be back?"

She snorted. "Soon's they let him out," she said.

"Is he—in jail?"

She pushed past me to get to the door. "No," she said. "He's in hospital."

"Are you his wife?" I stepped quickly in after her, before she could close the door in my face. Inside, the place was surprisingly comfortable-looking, if a little threadbare. Lush green plants filled the few windows and most of the corners, some under special grow lights.

She laughed sourly. "No," she said. "His sister. What *do* you want, anyway?"

She looked as hard and bleak as the neighborhood, a woman of about my age but with the look of someone life hasn't been good to. I met her suspicious gray eyes and decided to tell her the simple truth.

"I'm looking for Tom Carter," I said. "Rick's buddy. They were—"

"I know T. C. Why are you looking for him?"

What the hell, I thought. The woman was a complete stranger. And confession was supposed to be good for the soul.

"We're—old friends," I said. "More than just friends, actually. He's disappeared somewhere, and I'm worried about him, and mad at him, too."

Her narrow mouth slanted in a caustic smile. "Wouldn't be the first time he's had a woman on his trail feeling that way," she said. "Although you must be more persistent than most, if you got this far."

She didn't know where T. C. was, she told me. But she also told me some other things that caught my attention.

Her name was Pruitt, she said, Sally Pruitt. She was looking after Rick's plants while he was in the hospital.

I started to be more interested when she told me Rick had been badly beaten up the previous Monday afternoon. He'd been waylaid by a group of men on his way home from work.

There'd been no witnesses willing to identify the attackers. "And if Rick knows who they were, he's not saying," she added, her mouth pursed in disapproval or perhaps just sisterly concern.

On Monday, T. C. had stood me up for dinner.

On Tuesday, someone had overturned T. C.'s house and threatened me.

It seemed very unlikely that those events—and the beating of Rick Sayles—could be unconnected.

"Is there a chance I could visit Rick?" I asked.

She shook her head. "Not today," she said. "He's having a lot of tests, to make sure there was no lasting brain damage."

"Oh. So he was—"

She finished the sentence for me. "*Very* badly beaten up," she said. "The bastards kicked him around like a soccer ball. He's still a little disoriented, and it's been five days since it happened."

I started to feel a little queasy. If T. C. had encountered the same men—if he'd been in the wrong place—

"If you want to know, I have my suspicions about who did it," Sally Pruitt continued, as she moved to the kitchen sink and started running water into a plastic watering can that had been sitting on the counter. "The cops never tracked down the guy who started that bar fight. But I think it was this guy Rick fired at work. Rick's a construction foreman, or was, before he got arrested."

"I thought he was a pilot," I said.

"He used to be. He still has his license. But he doesn't fly much any more, just when T. C. manages to talk him into it. No, he's in construction. He fired this guy—and my guess the guy got his friends together to beat Rick up."

"Why now, after almost a year?"

"Rick was away." She started moving from window to window, watering Rick Sayles' unexpected garden. "He got a good job in Connecticut over the winter. They said he had to have steady work if he was going to get parole. He only came back because the job was over and—well, T. C. was out of prison. The two of them—"

She shook her head tightly. "They were always like brothers," she said. "Always together, always up to something.

Twenty years T. C. was gone in Alaska, and when as he came back, it was like they'd never been apart."

And Rick's sister didn't like it, I thought. T. C. was like that—he inspired resentment as well as devotion.

"They even look alike, you know," she added. "Same kind of hair, same kind of moustache. Same stupid grin. Twin terrors, guys used to call them in the Air Force."

Something was nagging at me as she spoke. "Wait a minute," I said. "You don't happen to have a picture of Rick handy, do you?"

"There's a picture of both of them together. It's one of Rick's prize possessions. Here, I'll get it."

By the time she brought the framed black and white photograph from the bureau in the apartment's single bedroom, the vague idea pushing at the back of my mind was starting to form into something more concrete.

The picture solidified it.

I should be on my way home by now, I knew. I still had to go shopping before I could begin to bake for Hannah's shower in the evening. And, although I was self-employed and technically free to come and go as I pleased, I didn't have unlimited time to spend in pursuit of old flames and unsolved mysteries.

But the idea of solving this one—of finding actual proof that the explanation taking shape in my mind might be true—was too tempting to resist.

Despite the fact that Rick Sayles' phone had been disconnected, there was still a copy of the Boston phone book sitting on his kitchen counter. It would give me the address I needed, I thought. If I made just one more stop, I might be able to clear this whole thing up.

"Would you mind," I said very slowly, "if I borrowed this picture for a few hours?"

The rain was ending by the time I got back to the subway. After the long walk to the bus, though, followed by an unwanted shower from a passing car driving too fast through a puddle, I was soaked. I was still wearing work clothes from the day before, and I felt anything but elegant as I got onto the subway at Davis Square.

I felt even scruffier when I got off again at Park Street in downtown Boston. At lunch time, the downtown area was crowded with people in business suits, all hurrying in search of food.

Food wasn't what I was after, although my stomach was hinting that it wasn't a bad idea. I looked at the address I'd copied from Rick Sayles' phone book and checked it against the Boston street map I'd brought with me from the truck.

Literacy Volunteers of Massachusetts had its offices in the center of the old downtown area. I turned down School Street off Tremont, passing King's Chapel on the corner and the old Boston City Hall just below it. A block away the new City Hall loomed over the open modern expanse of Government Center Plaza, but here the buildings were still packed close together as they'd been in the eighteenth and nineteenth centuries when most of Boston was built.

Court Square was tucked in behind the old City Hall. The Boston School Committee building filled most of the space in the square, but in one of the buildings around the edges, I finally found the address I was looking for.

The Literacy Volunteers of Massachusetts office was on the fifth floor. I entered a small waiting area and looked around, not seeing anyone at first.

After a moment, though, a woman's voice called from one of the inner offices that she would be with me in just a moment. I took a seat on the black leather sofa, because my feet were starting to complain about the amount of walking I'd done since morning.

A bookcase to my left held rows of reading material, including a lot of illustrated magazines. Across from me, an open door led into a room with a couple of computers and some other high-tech office equipment in it.

I knew LVM coordinated the local efforts of several Literacy Volunteers affiliates in the state, and I gathered, from the posters on the walls around me, that the program also trained tutors and supported new adult learners. Looking at the computers in the narrow room opposite me, I realized that it probably wasn't enough just to be book-literate any more. Computer literacy was a whole new field, one that made it even more important to master reading and writing.

And as far as computers went, I was a sub-beginner. I was pondering this view of myself when the woman from the inner office came out to greet me.

"I'm sorry, she's at a meeting," the woman at the front desk said when I'd explained who I was looking for. "She'll be back about three. Was she expecting you?"

I looked at my watch. I still hadn't baked a single one of the goodies I'd promised Hannah. And by the time I got back to where I'd parked, I was going to be contending with the start of Friday's rush-hour traffic. I didn't have time to spend waiting.

I decided to try the honest approach that had worked with Rick Sayles' sister. Maybe I could find out where the Literacy Volunteer staffer's meeting was, and intercept her.

"I know this sounds strange," I said to the woman at the desk, "but I towed your colleague's car last weekend when she was trying to get to the city for your conference."

The woman showed no surprise. "I know," she said. "She told us the whole story." She frowned at the "Henry's Towing" badge on the front of my damp green work shirt. "She said her auto plan would pay for the towing, though. Was there some problem—"

"No problem at all. Not with the bill, that is. I *do* have a slight problem with a missing person. Did your colleague tell you she ended up getting a ride with a friend of mine?"

"She did more than tell us." A smile lit the woman's face. "She brought him in to get him some coffee. We were all glad he rescued her—especially me. I'd have gotten stuck filling that workshop slot if she hadn't made it in time, and I wasn't anywhere near prepared to do it."

"So you actually saw the man who gave her a ride?"

"Oh, yes. I chatted with him, in fact."

I felt my hopes rising. "Do you think you would recognize him if you saw his picture?"

For the first time she looked a little suspicious. "Is there some kind of legal question here?" she asked. "Because I'm not sure I should—"

I could understand her hesitation. From my limited acquaintance with our local literacy program I knew that Literacy Volunteers specialized in tutoring adults. I could imagine that the people who came to Literacy Volunteers for help were frequently concerned about confidentiality. The staff member's response to my question was automatic, no doubt prompted by caution about other people's personal affairs.

So I chose my own next words with caution, too. "There are lots of legal questions involved," I said. "But I'm not taking sides on any of them. I'm concerned about a friend, that's all.

"If you're willing to point out to me the man you chatted with at the conference last weekend, I promise I'll forget we ever had this conversation. And if you need a character witness to vouch for my honesty, I'm sure Barbara Kenney would do it. She taught me back in second grade that you should always keep your promises."

Mrs. Kenney was the founder of the Orange-Athol branch of Literacy Volunteers, and it was a name well-known at LVM, so it did brighten the woman's face.

"All right," she said finally. "Let's see the picture."

I pulled the photograph of T. C. and his friend Rick out of my purse and gave it to her. She frowned.

"These two must be brothers," she said.

They might as well be, I almost replied. I didn't say anything, though. I was too busy waiting to see which face her hovering forefinger would eventually come down on.

When she made her choice, there was no hesitation in her tone. "That's the man who gave me the ride," she said firmly. "I'm sure of it."

And that made me sure, too, that my conjectures were on the right track. Because the man she'd picked was *not* Tom Carter, but his old friend Rick Sayles.

NINE

"Two each of the lemon-curd and custard tarts, please," I said. "And four of the cheesecake ones."

The woman picked up a new box and reached into the glass display case. In the back of my mind I could already hear Hannah's pleased reaction, which would no doubt turn very quickly to dismay when she realized what I'd resorted to.

Traffic on the way out of Boston had been even worse than usual. I'd gotten stuck in construction near Leominster and Fitchburg, which held me up for nearly forty-five minutes. I was still wearing my badly-wrinkled work clothes, and I knew my hair needed some attention if I was going to make a civilized impression at the baby shower.

That left me no time at all to bake. I'd admitted that to myself at about the time I'd finally cleared the construction traffic. Fortunately, the thought of Yankee Strudel in New Salem entered my mind at about the same time.

"We also have some very fresh cookies," the owner told me. "I like to make old-fashioned American recipes, like brambles and hermits and—"

Henry's mother had always made hermits. I loved them, but I hadn't forgotten Hannah's reaction to the idea of homemade cookies.

"Maybe some other time," I said.

The little bakery had opened several years earlier and had flourished by supplying a mouth-watering array of desserts. I knew the owner frequently catered special events, because I'd been to a fiftieth wedding anniversary the year before where the hit of the party had been the trays of delicacies supplied by Yankee Strudel.

The business also had a retail store on Route 202 in New Salem. Open on Fridays, Saturdays, and Sundays, the little shop was just big enough for a couple of chairs and a glass case filled with exactly the kind of treats Hannah was fondly imagining I'd been laboring over for the past several days.

Instead, I'd been chasing clues and towing cars. Thank goodness for specialty businesses like Yankee Strudel, I thought.

"I said I'd bring dessert," I muttered. "And I will, damn it."

"Excuse me?" The woman's face appeared over the glass counter top.

"Nothing," I said. "I've been wondering—is there *anything* besides chocolate in those truffle brownies?"

She smiled. "Very little," she said. "We use just enough flour to hold them together."

I'd suspected that was the case. "You'd better give me half a dozen," I said.

Hannah's friends—calorie-counters all—would no doubt look askance at the sinfully dark chocolate squares. But I was willing to bet there wouldn't be a single brownie left by the end of the evening.

I sighed when I thought about how far away that was likely to be. Hannah and her friend Nerissa had invited everyone they knew, and that meant lots of gifts and lots of party games—the kind I was hardly in the mood for.

I wanted to be following up the clues I'd discovered over the past two days. I'd put together a partial picture of what T. C. was in the middle of, but there were still pieces missing. If I could spend the evening making phone calls, instead of making little hats out of gift-wrap bows—

I tried to put the thought out of my head. I'd already stretched my promise to my daughter far enough—especially given the fact that I'd just assured the woman at Literacy Volunteers I was the kind of person who knew promises were supposed to be kept.

So I did my best to put my remaining questions aside as I watched Yankee Strudel's owner wrapping up my purchases.

Unfortunately—or fortunately, depending on your viewpoint—chance stepped in at that point.

The little bell over the door rang just as I was debating whether to get a couple of cookies for me and Davis to snack on later. I turned and saw a man who looked vaguely familiar, followed by a casually-dressed couple in their forties. The woman was petite and blonde; her companion, who was wearing a Dallas Cowboys jersey, was much taller and dark-haired.

"I knew she would still have some," the first man was saying as the three of them entered. "By Sunday, they're usually gone, but Friday is a good bet."

The couple stepped closer to the glass counter and made appropriately awed noises at the display of goodies. "I love coming out here to eat," the man said. "I thought the two-pound prime rib at the Homestead was the pinnacle, but now—"

He leaned over next to the woman, examining the Yankee Strudel's wares enthusiastically.

"This is Janice and H. C. Hansen," the man said to the bakery's owner. "They're up from the Cape for the weekend. I met them when they stopped for lunch in the restaurant next door and talked them into coming in here for dessert. I told them your cheesecake tarts were about the best thing the North Quabbin has to offer tourists—besides our views of the sky, of course."

I'd finally identified the man. He was the owner's husband, and something of a local—even national—celebrity because of an organization he'd founded called For Spacious Skies.

For Spacious Skies was dedicated to a single principle: that paying attention to the sky is good for you. In the philosophy of this latter-day Thoreau, simply observing the sky is a way to focus your mind beyond the tangle of details that all of us are tied up in. If we took more time just to tilt our heads back and watch the sky our thinking would expand, our sense of our place in the natural world would be enhanced, and we would be able to see life—literally—in a broader perspective.

At the moment, it was a seductive idea. And I couldn't help wondering whether all the time T. C. had spent in airplanes had enhanced his own leave-the-details-behind approach to life.

Had looking at the world from several thousand feet up reinforced his belief that the details just weren't worth worrying about?

He'd left more than a few details dangling behind him when he disappeared this time. I still hadn't quite forgiven him for that—or for trying to make me an unwitting party to the trick he'd attempted to play on his parole officer.

And until I knew *why* he'd done it—

"There are lots of good places to walk right around here, if you're staying in the area."

The deep voice of the man from For Spacious Skies recalled me to the present. His wife was holding out my boxes of goodies and waiting for me to pay her.

As I dug in my purse for my wallet, I heard the visiting woman say, "We're staying with a friend in Athol. But we did want to do some hiking around the Quabbin Reservoir."

"There's a wonderful view of the reservoir from a trail just up the road." I couldn't help joining the conversation, thinking of what a good time T. C. and I had had prowling around New Salem a week earlier.

From stray comments the couple had been making to each other, I gathered they were celebrating their recent wedding. I felt a sudden pang of envy—not for their married state so much as their obvious enjoyment of each other's company and the fact that they had each other to share this weekend in the country.

The owner's husband was nodding at my words. "That lookout is a good place to start," he said. "You can see a big slice of the sky from up there. I was out there a couple of nights ago, in fact. Somebody was practicing aerobatic routines out over the reservoir—it was quite spectacular."

The news brought me up short.

"Do you know anything about aerobatics?" I asked.

He frowned at me. "A little," he said. "Why?"

"I just wondered whether the pilot you saw was any good."

He nodded. "He was *very* good," he said. "In fact, he looked like he was just out there for the hell of it, doing loops and rolls for fun. You know, kind of a tribute to the setting sun. Like he was enjoying being out there in the sky. At least, that's how I interpreted it."

I couldn't think of a better description of the way Tom Carter felt about flying.

Was it T. C. that the man from For Spacious Skies had seen?

Was it possible he'd sneaked back into the area after his latest adventure?

If he was—

And if he was hiding—

"The airport," I said out loud. "He would hide at the airport."

"I beg your pardon?"

The bakery owner was still waiting patiently for me to pay her. I fished the money out of my wallet, shaking my head as I handed it across the counter. I couldn't possibly explain to these near-strangers how many lines of thought were crisscrossing my own personal sky. But before long, I hoped, I was going to be able to explain it all with perfect clarity to myself.

The phone was ringing as I stepped into my house. "If that's Tina, I'm just getting out of the shower," Davis shouted from the bathroom.

"Get out in a hurry, then," I called back. "I've got to take a shower, too."

The voice on the other end of the phone was Hannah's, though. "How are you getting here?" she wanted to know.

"How do you think? The tow truck, of course."

"Oh, *Mom*." I could almost see her rolling her eyes. "You can't!"

"Why not?" I set the Yankee Strudel boxes down on the counter and carried the cordless phone into my bedroom, where I started pulling things out of my closet.

"Well, for one thing there'll be no room to park it. We have so many other cars coming. And for another—"

"Don't tell me. I'll embarrass you in front of your friends." I grabbed a pair of tan trousers that I knew looked good with my one dressy jacket. I rejected it a moment later, though. Hannah wouldn't be truly happy unless I showed up in a skirt.

And despite my moments of contrariness, I did want to make my daughter happy. I felt a little guilty about the store-bought goodies, although they were as close to homemade as store-bought would ever get. I reached for a white blouse with round pearl buttons—bought last year for a friend's daughter's wedding—and a bright red pleated skirt. They would do, I thought.

"I'll get Nerissa to come and pick you up." Hannah sounded brisk and practical, as though she'd had this backup plan up her sleeve already. "Can you be ready in fifteen minutes?"

"Make it half an hour." I scrambled around in the back of the closet and found the pair of red pumps I'd bought to go with the skirt. With some red and gold beads and some attention to my hair, I thought, I ought to look like a reasonable facsimile of a socially-acceptable matron.

A last-minute phone call from Mr. Magoo didn't do anything for my frame of mind. Neither did the fact that this time, when I repeated that I still didn't know where T. C. was, I knew I was on the edge of telling him a lie.

"Well, if you hear from him—"

A horn tooted from the driveway, polite yet insistent. "I've got to run," I told T. C.'s parole officer. "It's been nice talking to you."

I hung up before he could tell me he didn't like my attitude. I could feel my irritation starting to get the better of me again, and I knew I couldn't let that happen if I was going to play the gracious hostess at Hannah's.

I think I did a creditable job. The general pleasure at the delicious desserts from Yankee Strudel seemed to soften some of Hannah's disappointment that I hadn't, after all, spent a couple of days up to my elbows in puff pastry.

I made polite small-talk with her friends and their mothers and even led one of the tours of the baby's new room, where I carefully pointed out the fact that the colors in the wallpaper border would coordinate with either pink or blue sheets.

By seven-thirty, I was bored silly.

Hannah had hired a photographer, Robert Mayer from Athol, to take a group portrait of herself and her friends. Bob arrived just before seven, and Hannah immediately began stressing to him that she wanted this to be just an informal portrait, while at the same time rattling off a list of suggestions about where to pose and how the light should be.

"Hi, Rita." Bob Mayer recognized me as he followed Hannah into the crowded living room. "How're you doing?"

I gave him the same bright social smile I'd been using all evening. "Great," I said. "How come they never serve beer at baby showers?"

He laughed. "I didn't *think* this looked like your kind of scene," he said.

"Come on, everybody," Hannah was calling brightly. "And the pregnant lady gets to sit in the middle, on the sofa. I have every intention of staying as comfortable and as close to the ground as possible from now until I give birth, unlike that woman in Los Angeles last week."

It hit me like a bolt from the blue.

"Holy cow," I said, suddenly standing still.

"Come on, Mom." Out of the corner of my eye I could see Hannah waving me over. "You sit next to me."

I didn't move. I was thinking hard, trying to recall the news story I'd read while waiting for Davis at the bookstore a few days earlier.

"Mom..."

Where had that flight originated? Had the story said?

If it was what I was thinking—

"Do you still have this week's issues of the *Daily News*?" I asked Hannah. "Or did you throw them out already?"

She looked at me as though I'd finally and completely lost my mind. "They're in the recycling box," she said. "Are you feeling all right, Mom?"

"No. Yes. Look, I've got to—"

Hannah's friend Nerissa got an arm around my shoulders before I could head for the kitchen, gently steering me into the middle of the picture. "There we go, Mrs. Magritte," she said, in the soothing voice people use with elderly people and lunatics. "This won't take long."

It seemed to take forever. I guess I smiled—at least, in the finished picture I have a smile on my face. But my mind was a thousand miles away. The moment the final flash went off, I was on my feet and into the kitchen.

The week's papers were neatly bundled into the blue box under Hannah's sink. I cut the string with a knife and dug through the stack until I found the one I wanted.

"Moscow," I said, when I turned up the right article. "I was *right*."

I was also stranded. I'd already started for the door, intending to head straight for the airport in search of the man whose mysterious disappearance I'd now fully unraveled, when it struck me that I had no way to get there.

"Are you driving back to Athol?" I asked Bob Mayer, who was packing up his equipment at the kitchen table.

He nodded. "Need a lift?"

"Is there any way in the world you could drop me at the Orange Airport?" I asked.

Hannah was in the doorway, already protesting. Her friend Nerissa was trying to reason with me. Someone else was asking whether it was time to start opening the presents.

But I felt I'd done my duty at the shower, and there was an official photograph to prove it. Ripping the article about the midair birth out of the newspaper, I called my apologies over my shoulder as I followed Bob Mayer out to his car.

TEN

It wasn't just any car—it was a vintage white Volvo, gleaming with a recent paint job.

"All right, what are you up to now?" Bob wanted to know, as he urged it into fourth gear along North Main Street in Orange.

"If I told you even half of it, you wouldn't believe me," I said. "In fact, I'm not sure *I* believe it yet. I'm on my way to find out whether what I think is going on is actually true or not."

Bob laughed again. "Sounds like a Rita Magritte story, all right," he said. I noticed him glancing in his rearview mirror, then frowning. "I wish this guy would get off my bumper," he said. "This is a curvy road."

When he made almost the same comment several miles later, as we approached the airport, I turned to look myself.

And saw a man with dark curly hair glaring at me. Under the street light in the center of Orange, I could see the Red Sox logo on his red wool jacket.

"Oh, shoot," I said.

Bob gave me a sharp look. "Friend of yours?" he said.

"Not exactly."

I knew now that the man who'd threatened me at T. C.'s house was *not* T. C.'s friend Rick Sayles. That was the good news.

The bad news was that the guy in the Red Sox jacket was most likely the one who'd started that bar fight a year ago—and the same one who'd returned with his buddies to beat Rick Sayles up so badly he'd ended up in hospital.

We'd already passed my own house, so there was no way to pretend I'd simply been heading home. Bob was steering the Volvo into the airport entrance. And that meant there was no good way to shake off the bully behind us before we got close to T. C., assuming T. C. was even there.

Ten minutes earlier I'd been eager to find him, eager to confront him with the story I'd finally pieced together. Now I was starting to hope he would be nowhere to be found, for his own safety.

Being T. C., of course, he was right there in full view.

I saw him as we approached the control building. He had a dark green baseball cap pulled over his gray hair, and he was leaning over the engine of the airplane he'd used when he'd taken me flying. I knew the familiar outline of him immediately, though—the angle of his hips, the cocky stance of his whole body.

If I'd seen his friend Rick out of the cockpit of the plane or the cab of the pickup truck last week, I'd have recognized earlier that the two of them had pulled a switch on me, I thought. But they'd taken care that I'd caught only glimpses of Rick from the shoulders up, and that his voice had always been disguised by the noise of an engine.

The resemblance between them was good enough—and I'd been trusting enough—that they'd managed to fool me. When Mr. Magoo had asked me when I'd last seen T. C., I'd answered "Saturday morning," believing I was telling the truth.

If T. C.'s plan had gone the way he'd intended, that alibi would have been enough to cover the unauthorized long-distance trip he'd made over the weekend. No doubt he'd honestly been planning to be back in time for dinner with me Monday evening. But things had gone wrong. And I'd finally figured out how.

There wasn't time to dwell on that as Bob Mayer and I approached the low brick building at the Orange Airport.

The car behind us suddenly veered around Bob's white Volvo, screeching up to the building before Bob could do anything more than just give a startled shout.

I heard him shout again as I launched myself out of the Volvo in hot pursuit. Bob's door slammed just after mine did, but by then I was already running as fast as my leather pumps would allow toward the runway beyond the building.

I didn't get there fast enough. T. C. saw the dark-haired man approaching and quickly slammed the cover over the plane's engine. The machine must have been all ready to go, judging by how quickly he got himself into the pilot's seat and started the plane moving out onto the runway.

He was planning to disappear again. It is his stock in trade, after all.

And given the savage way his best buddy had been treated by this same man—and the fact that T. C. had already served jail time for fighting with the guy—I didn't blame him.

Besides, there was nothing I could do except watch as the little plane lifted up and soared into the darkening evening sky. He didn't seem to have noticed me. Between the fact that I was all dressed up and the absence of my familiar tow truck, he'd probably figured I was just some stranger.

And maybe I was. I fought back a lump of disappointment in my throat as I watched T. C. flying away from me for what might very well be the final time.

The man in the Red Sox jacket wasn't wasting any time standing around being sentimental. I heard his roar of frustration as his quarry outdistanced him. Then he stalked back to his car and got in, clearly intending to disappear in the opposite direction.

I couldn't let that happen. This man had been responsible for beating Rick Sayles. And while he was on the loose, T. C. would almost certainly continue to keep his distance from me and everything else connected with his old home. If there was any hope of really resolving this whole adventure, it had to start with bringing the stranger to justice.

And nobody seemed to be interested in doing that except me.

Bob Mayer's shiny white car was still parked next to the airport building. Bob himself was standing next to it, watching, but I could see that the keys were still in the ignition.

"I have to borrow your car." I slid into the driver's seat over his protests. "Listen, get into the building and call the police, all right? Tell them—well, just tell them to get down here."

I didn't wait to explain it in any more detail. The Orange Police Department was just down the road. With luck they would be able to send a cruiser before Raspy-Voice and I had gotten too far away.

It almost didn't work.

The guy in the Red Sox jacket drove like the proverbial bat out of hell. He knew I was behind him and did his best to out-distance me as we careened onto Daniel Shays Highway at the end of Airport Road.

The old Volvo hadn't been designed for high-speed chases. And despite my nerve in "borrowing" it out from under Bob Mayer's nose, I really didn't want to do anything to damage the vehicle that was clearly his pride and joy.

When we reached Route 2, I was already lagging behind.

Once Raspy-Voice hit the highway, I knew he would be able to make better time than I could.

But he never got onto the highway.

I thought I saw him slowing to turn onto the entrance ramp ahead of me. Out of nowhere, though, I heard the sound of an engine. And a moment later a bright blue and yellow airplane swooped down and buzzed the car, coming in so close it almost seemed the plane wouldn't be able to clear the Route 2 overpass as T. C. lifted up again.

It did clear, of course. T. C. was the best there was when it came to fancy flying.

But why the hell had he come back?

I watched Raspy-Voice's car veer wildly to the left as he tried to avoid the plane's sudden descent. Horns blared in the other lane, and the car fishtailed as its driver got it back under control and jumped on the gas.

By that time I'd nearly caught up. We shot south along Daniel Shays Highway at a speed I didn't even want to think about.

The car ahead of me was gaining ground again as we hit the open stretch of road approaching South Main Street.

But then the plane dive-bombed us a second time. And Raspy-Voice—who obviously didn't know how much faith to put in T. C.'s skill—panicked as the blue and yellow streak blazed down out of the sky, heading straight for the car's windshield.

I thought I could actually hear the driver's panicky yell. His car swerved to the right, then the left. When he got it back under control, his nerve seemed shaken. He took the right turn onto South Main Street, but his steering was erratic, and he came close to running off the road altogether at the sharp curve.

"Come on, T. C.," I said out loud. "One more and you've got him."

I still couldn't imagine what had prompted T. C. to turn around in mid-flight and come back. He'd been heading into the wild blue yonder—I'd seen him with my own eyes. And he had no way of knowing I was the one in the white Volvo. I might be a crony of Raspy-Voice, for all T. C. knew.

Yet there he was, coming in for another pass. I slacked off on the gas, giving him lots of room.

The other vehicle was barreling toward the Route 2 entrance off South Main Street. The only thing in the way was Route 2 itself where it crossed the road we were on.

T. C. didn't let that slow him down. He timed his move perfectly. As Raspy-Voice hauled his wheel around to make the turn, the little plane came screaming down, missing the bridge by mere feet, and carving a sharp curve out of the air right in front of the turning car.

It was more than the driver could deal with. I watched as the car shot off the entrance ramp and into the field beyond, leaving long dark furrows behind it where its tires ate into rain-softened ground.

Behind me I could hear sirens. Either Bob Mayer's emergency call had finally produced some results, I thought, or someone had reported that a single-engine airplane was apparently strafing the roads around the Orange Airport.

The plane was gone by the time the police arrived. I watched it go, almost more fascinated by the disappearing blue and yellow dot in the sky than by the struggle as a pair of Orange police officers caught up with Raspy-Voice and wrestled him to soggy ground near the cloverleaf.

It was finally over, I thought. And I knew what had happened and why.

But I still didn't know whether I was ever going to see Tom Carter again.

ELEVEN

"So what did they finally arrest Raspy-Voice for?" Davis held out a bite of hamburger for the dog, who accepted it daintily, then swallowed it without even chewing.

"I never did hear the whole list. It turned out he'd been running an operation that skimmed materials from construction sites where he worked—that's why T. C.'s friend Rick fired him."

"And then he came looking for Rick to get even."

"Right. But T. C. was there, and the two of them were more than he could handle. He skipped out of the fight early, leaving T. C. and Rick to get into all sorts of trouble for fighting with the cops who'd come to settle things down. And then he just bided his time until Rick came back to the area and T. C. got out of jail."

"He sounds like a walking definition of 'vengeful,'" said Tina, who'd joined us for Sunday night's dinner.

"He was." I took a bite of my own burger and reflected, soberly, that both T. C. and I had been lucky. I'd gotten off with just a warning, and T. C. had managed to elude Raspy-Voice—whose real name turned out to be Chuck Naylor—until two nights before.

"So the arrest sheet included some old theft charges stemming from his construction days, plus assault and battery on Rick Sayles, plus breaking and entering at T. C.'s place."

"Not to mention kicking the stuffing out of you." Davis looked reproachful as he got up to put a couple more burgers onto my backyard grill.

I stretched my arms over my head. "That's the advantage of having a lot of stuffing," I said. "I feel fine now, Davis. You don't have to get all motherly."

Tina smiled, but Davis didn't look amused. "And you complain about T. C. not telling you what's going on," he said. "If you'd thought to mention to me last week that you'd been threatened—"

Davis was right about T. C. not telling me what was going on. I hadn't seen or heard from him in the two days since Chuck Naylor had been arrested. For all I knew, T. C. might be back in jail—but if he was, he hadn't seen fit to let me know about it.

Tina seemed to notice the faint bitterness in my voice. Smoothing things over was second nature to her, and she said quickly, "But at least you know now why he vanished, right?"

Davis shook his head. "Man," he said, "I can't believe that the woman who had the baby on the airplane turned out to be T. C.'s *daughter*. How did you put that together, Rita?"

"Slowly." I finished my hamburger and leaned back in my lawn chair. "I didn't know at first that T. C. even *had* a daughter. It seemed farfetched that his daughter in Moscow and the woman from Moscow who'd had her baby in flight would be the same person—until I realized that T. C. disappeared at exactly the time when that woman was due to land in L. A."

"So she was coming to the U. S.?" Tina asked.

I shook my head. "She was going to South America," I said. "Her husband is there—he's an engineer. But T. C., who'd been keeping in touch with his daughter over the past few years, found out she had a six-hour layover in L. A. It was the nearest he was likely to get to her for a while, and his only chance to visit her without leaving the country."

"And getting a visa was going to be a problem, when he wasn't even supposed to leave the county while he was on parole," Davis put in.

"Right. So he and his old buddy—who's cut from the same cloth, from what his sister told me—hatched this plan."

The plan had been a simple one. Rick Sayles had bought himself a return plane ticket to Los Angeles for the same day that T. C.'s daughter would be flying into the west coast.

Meanwhile, T. C. had been cultivating me, setting up a romantic routine of taking sunset flights together every evening. When he'd seemed a little distracted on Friday evening, I'd readily ascribed it to his concern over the instrument panel, never dreaming that the man under the goggles and hat wasn't my old boyfriend but his accomplice, who'd always looked enough like him to pass for his brother.

"Rick stuck around that night, just in case anyone happened to go by T. C.'s house, or in case Mr. Magoo called and wondered why nobody was home," I said. "And when I called the next morning, asking him for a favor, he said yes, because he was due to drive into Boston anyway. They'd set up the "visit" to Rick as a blind. The plan was for T. C. to fly back in on Sunday evening, drive back out to Athol, and have nobody ever know he'd been to the other side of the country to see his long-lost daughter."

Two things had interfered with the plan. First, the vengeful Chuck Naylor had come looking for the two men he bore a grudge against.

And then T. C.'s daughter had given birth en route to L. A.

"He couldn't stand to leave her," I said, repeating what I'd heard through the police grapevine. "She was alone, scared, in a country where she couldn't speak the language—"

Not that T. C. had been able to help there, despite his last-minute intentions to learn Russian before his visit. But there had been some complications during the in-flight birth, and both mother and baby had been in rough shape for a day or two. T. C. had stayed by his daughter's side, and I couldn't say I blamed him for doing it.

I *did* have some thoughts about the cynical way he'd set me up to be his alibi, but I didn't voice those to Davis and Tina.

"He managed to get back on Wednesday," I said instead. "But when he saw the state of his house—and recognized Chuck Naylor hanging around the place—he knew he was in a whole different kind of trouble. He tried to contact Rick Sayles and learned what Naylor and his buddies had done to him. That made T. C. think it was even smarter to stay underground until Naylor had left the area."

"'Underground' is the wrong term for it," Davis said.

I nodded. "He was hiding at the airport, because it would give him the best possible escape route—the sky."

If he hadn't given in to the temptation to go flying on Wednesday evening—and if there hadn't happened to be an unusually acute sky-watcher down in New Salem who'd noticed him—I might not have figured out where T. C. was.

And once I had, I'd led the danger straight to him.

"There's still one thing I don't understand." Tina shook her head as Davis offered her a second hamburger. Chili Dog perked up, scenting leftovers. "What made him suddenly start dive-bombing Chuck Naylor's car like that? I thought you said he took one look at the guy and took off."

"He did." I had to smile myself at the way my interference had turned out for the best after all. "The man who'd driven me to the airport—Bob Mayer—is a photographer. But he wasn't always a photographer. He used to be—"

"An air traffic controller."

The deep voice from the corner of the house surprised all three of us—four, in fact, if you count Chili Dog's startled *woof*.

Tom Carter, lanky as ever and twice as handsome, was leaning on the side of the building, with a bottle in one hand and a box in the other.

He shoved himself upright as we all turned to stare at him. I wondered how long he'd been standing there listening. He was a sneaky old feline, I thought. And he didn't even have the grace to look concerned about having recently used up at least one more of his remaining lives.

"First I knew about it was this voice on the radio," he said, approaching the circle of chairs around the grill.

"I was monitoring the Unicom frequency—all pilots do it in the vicinity of an airport, just to check what traffic's out there and what the conditions are and so on. Suddenly there's this guy telling me that Rita Magritte was in a white Volvo heading east on Airport Road and that she seemed to be in some kind of hot water."

The mystery voice had belonged to Bob Mayer. After calling the Orange police as I'd asked him to do, he'd realized that the blue and yellow airplane that had just taken off seemed to be at the center of whatever was going on. With his background in air traffic control, he'd known how to use the Orange Airport's equipment to contact the aircraft.

And once he had, T. C. had realized what must be happening. "I recognized Naylor's car," he said as he set the bottle down on the picnic table.

I could see it was red wine, and not cheap stuff, either, judging by my quick glance at the label. "But I knew Naylor was out there looking for me. And I knew Rita was crazy enough to keep chasing him until she caught him, which wasn't going to be good news for Rita. The guy had a gun, Rita—didn't you even consider that?"

I hadn't until a police officer had told me about it after the chase. "I was just trying to get things cleared up," I said. "That's all."

"'That's all.'" T. C. shook his silver head. "Damn, woman, don't you have *any* sense?"

"You're asking *me* that?" I stared at him. "If you'd been less of a daredevil in the first place—"

Davis had been busy wolfing down his second burger, much to Chili Dog's disappointment. The boy stood up, holding out a hand to Tina. "Come on," he said. "We wanted to get down to Ralph Longg's in time for the concert, remember?"

It was the first I'd heard of any concert, although I knew there was live music at Ralph's on Sundays. I suspected Davis just wanted to be out of the way of any fireworks that were about to go off between me and T. C. And judging from the way Chili Dog slunk into his doghouse when the teenagers had gone, he felt much the same way.

If they'd all stuck around, I could have told them that fireworks were different in middle age. They were just as exciting, but real life was always a little closer to hand to temper the thrill.

I could fall in love with Tom Carter all over again, I thought, as I watched him settle his rangy frame into the chair next to mine. But it would be on my terms.

Adventure and routine had taken on new meaning for me over the past few days. Adventure hadn't lost any of its allure, but I wasn't going to sit around looking at the sky waiting for it to drop into my lap. As T. C. had just pointed out, I was capable of generating plenty of adventure all on my own.

And routine no longer looked like something I needed to escape from. I had to admit it—part of me had enjoyed the tumult of the past few days. But now that it was all over, I was also enjoying sitting with my feet up on the chaise longue looking at the green calm of my own back yard. If T. C. wanted to play any role my life, he was going to have to accept that part of it, too.

Surprisingly, he seemed to be thinking along the very same lines.

"You know," he said, leaning back in his chair, "I've been talking to people for two solid days. Had to talk to the FAA about some things they weren't wild about—"

"It had nothing to do with buzzing bridges at low altitude, did it?"

He grinned. "Those boys got no sense of humor," he said. "And then I had to talk to Orange cops. And Athol cops. And state cops. And my daughter's mother, all the way from Russia, who thinks I'm somehow responsible for her little girl giving birth in midair. And then I had to talk to Rick's sister." His face clouded. "I don't know what I'm going to do if Rick's not okay."

"I know." I reached out and took his hand. I squeezed it tight. "I imagine you've had to do some talking with Mr. Magoo, too."

"Nope. Just listening. Mr. Magoo talks enough for two." He squeezed my hand in return, and turned to look at me. For once in his life, he looked utterly serious. "What I'm saying to you, Rita, is that I'm tired of talking. Tired of questions. And I wondered—would you be willing just to sit and *not* talk with me for a while?"

I thought about it. "I do have one question," I said.

"What's that?"

"What's in the box?"

He looked at the box he'd set on the picnic table. "Cookies," he said. "Old-fashioned American ones, the woman said. They're from—"

"I know where they're from. How about handing one over here?"

"That's two questions."

"I'll stop now. For a while."

He grinned faintly. "But only for a while. Right?"

"You said yourself, there's always a catch with me. Looks like you're finally just figuring out what that means."

In the trees between my yard and the river, a firefly flashed, and then another one. I couldn't tell—and didn't much care— whether this was high adventure or everyday routine. For the moment it was good enough just to be sitting in my yard with Tom Carter's hand in mine, eating old-fashioned cookies and watching the fireflies put on a show as the light slowly faded from the sky above us and the night rolled over the world again.